William C Higgins

Scaling the Eagle's Nest

The Life of Russell H. Conwell of Philadelphia

William C Higgins

Scaling the Eagle's Nest
The Life of Russell H. Conwell of Philadelphia

ISBN/EAN: 9783337008178

Printed in Europe, USA, Canada, Australia, Japan

Cover: Foto ©Raphael Reischuk / pixelio.de

More available books at **www.hansebooks.com**

The Life of Russell H. Conwell,

OF PHILADELPHIA.

BY

AN OLD ARMY COMRADE.

EDITED BY A. E. H.

PUBLISHED BY

JAMES D. GILL,

SPRINGFIELD, MASS.

PREFACE BY THE EDITOR.

In preparing this biography for the public, the editor, with the most valuable aid of friends, has enlarged and arranged the writings of Mr. Wm. C. Higgins of North Blandford, Mass., who was a soldier in Mr. Conwell's command during the war with the Southern Confederacy. Mr. Higgins was a most devoted friend of Mr. Conwell, and when a history of the Forty-sixth Massachusetts Volunteers was being compiled, Mr. Higgins volunteered to gather the facts of Mr. Conwell's life for publication, as a part of the history of that regiment. Mr. Higgins was a private soldier in that regiment, and Mr. Conwell was a captain at that time. But the collection of biographical material was too extensive for such a volume, and the idea of the publication in that form was abandoned.

Since Mr. Higgins' death, the growing fame of Mr. Conwell's orations, lectures and sermons has created a demand for a biography which the editor hesitatingly attempts in a measure to supply, by using all of Mr. Higgins' collection with many additions, and much re-

arrangement.   The editor has tried to preserve the form
of Mr. Higgins' narrative, and retains the personal pro-
noun of the biographer thoughout; although in many
places considerable new matter has been added by the
advice of friends.

The editor would also add the following copy of a
letter from Mr. Conwell, which will explain itself:—

[MR. CONWELL'S LETTER.]

GRACE BAPTIST CHURCH,
PHILADELPHIA, PA., Jan. 1, 1889.

Dear Friend: It was a surprise to me to learn how much
attention Comrade Higgins had given to an account of my
life.   I don't believe it would pay to publish it as a business
investment.   But I do feel a strange mingling of sadness
and gratitude when I think of his life-long friendship, and
the sorrow his death has awakened.   He was a good man.
God bless every one who loved him.   I am glad to know that
the profits of the publication, should there be any, are so
generously to be divided with his widow.   I should be glad
to give you any reasonable assistance my much crowded life
will permit.

Your friend as ever,

RUSSELL H. CONWELL.

INDEX.

CHAPTER I.

Parents—The hunter's discovery—The flock of sheep—
Climbing the old tree—Expedients and perseverance
—The victory.

ALTHOUGH I was probably acquainted with Russell H. Conwell from his birth, for I lived all his early years two miles from his home, in Worthington, Hampshire County, Massachusetts, yet I do not remember much of him during his earliest childhood.

His father Martin Conwell, and his mother Miranda Wickham Conwell were intimate acquaintances before their marriage.

Martin was one of my boyhood's playmates. His home from the time of his marriage was in a small, red, one and one-half story farm house, near a summit of a rugged part of that mountain region. Back of the old farm house and its out-buildings is a hill of rock, from which is a magnificent view of the deep valley leading through mountains seen forty miles away.

But the first time I saw Russell, which I now recall,

was when he was a shepherd boy, not over ten years old, watching his father's sheep along the jagged hillside included in his father's rocky possessions. I had been out hunting for wild bee trees with his uncle, and came out of the forest at the top of a high rock which forms a crest of the broken hill north of the Conwell homestead. It was a cool October day, and ten thousand colors ornamented the hills and valleys, and the distant mountain tops. I am often now reminded of that scene when I hear Mr. Conwell deliver an address, or read one of his books.

Russell was in charge of a flock of sheep, and I think he had a hard time to keep them in order among the high boulders, the steep ledges and the clumps of thick bushes. But just in front of, and out on a lower ledge or cliff, of the hill was a knotted, knarled and broken hemlock tree, which the storms had nearly killed. It must have been fifty feet high then, and some storm or stroke of lightning had broken off much of the top. There was only one limb which was left whole, and many of the others had been broken off close to the trunk, or splintered down. It was a craggy ruin of a great tree. It grew on a wide, barren rock, with the roots running away out to cracks for support. On the top of that tree, in the splintered and twisted crown, was an eagle's nest. A rude thing, built of awkward sticks, with a bunch of hay in the center. There was

Mr. Conwell's Birthplace.

no other tree near that old trunk, and alone it had withstood the storms for probably a half century after the woods were cleared.

"There's Russell climbing that tree !" said his uncle, Mr. Cole, who was with me. But I had to look several times and shade my eyes before I could see the boy, he was so small.

"What is that little fellow going to do now ?" I asked.

But Mr. Cole was as much puzzled as was I. Mr. Cole thought he had better call him down, for his parents would have been terribly frightened if they had seen that boy alone struggling to get up that tree. But we decided to sit down by the bushes and watch him, and see what he was trying to do. He did not discover us, and we sat there for two hours or more, watching his manœuvers. It was rich amusement, and we laughed till we cried. The sheep were browsing about the great rocks in the unfenced clearing, and knew his voice so well that in the midst of his struggles, if he saw any of the sheep going too far away he had only to call them by name, and they came slowly back nibbling at the bushes.

He was evidently after the eagle's nest, but there was not a man in the mountains who would have thought it possible to do anything else but to shoot it down. When we first saw him he was half way up the great tree, and was tugging away to get up by a broken limb which was swinging loosely about the trunk. For a long time he tried to break it off, but his little hand was too weak. Then he came down from knot to knot like a squirrel, and jumped to the ground and ran to his little jacket and took his jack-knife out of the pocket. Then he slowly clambered up again. When he reached the limb again, he clung to another limb with his left hand and threw one leg over a splintered knot and with the right hand hacked away with his knife.

"He will give it up," we both said.

But he did not. He chipped away until at last the limb fell to the ground. Then he pocketed his knife, and bravely strove to get up higher. It was a dizzy height even for a grown hunter, but the boy never looked down. He went on until he came to a place about ten feet below the nest, where there was a long, bare space on the trunk, with no limbs or knots to cling to. He was baffled then. We laughed under our breath as he looked on one side, then on the other. He looked up at the nest many times, tried to find some place to catch hold of the rough bark and sought closely for some rest to put his foot on higher up. But there was none. An eagle's nest was a rare thing to him, and he hugged the tree and thought. Suddenly he began hastily to descend again, and soon dropped to the ground. Away he ran down through the ravines, leaping the little streams and disappeared toward his home. We knew he would not leave the sheep long, so we sat still. It was but a few minutes before we saw his torn straw hat and blue shirt flitting about the rocks and bushes, and soon he came back to the tree. He called the sheep all to him and talked to them, and shook his finger at them, but we could not hear what he said.

Then he clambered up the tree again, dragging after him a long piece of his mother's clothes line. At one end of it he had tied a large stone, and it hindered his progress as it caught in the limbs and splinters. The wind blew his torn straw hat away down a side cliff, and he tore one side of his pants leg sadly. But he went on. When he got to the smooth place on the tree again, he fastened one end of the rope about his wrist, and then taking the stone which was fastened to the other end, he tried to throw it up over the nest. It was an awkward and a dangerous position, and the stone did not reach the top. Six or seven times he threw that stone up, and it fell short or went to one side, and nearly dragged him down as it fell.

"Let's stop him! Let's stop him!" I said.

But Mr. Cole said, "Let him try once more."

The little boy felt for his knife again, and opened it with his teeth as he held on, and hauling the rope up, cut off a part of it. Then he threw a short piece around the tree and tied himself with it to the tree. Then he could lean back for a longer throw. So he tied the rope to his hand again, and threw the stone with all his energy. It went straight as an arrow. It drew the rope squarely over the nest and fell down the other side of the tree. After quite a struggle he reached around the tree for the stone, and tied that end of the rope to a long broken limb. When he drew the other end of the rope which had been fastened to his hand, it broke down the sides of the nest at the top of the tree, and an old bird arose from the nest with a wild scream.

We had supposed the nest was deserted until that moment. I was afraid the eagle would show fight, and we put our guns in order to bring her down if she came back to attack the boy. But she swooped down about the place but twice, and then flew away off to a grove on another hill.

Then Russell loosed the rope which held him to the tree, and pulling himself up with his hands on the scaling line, digging his bare toes, heels and knees at times into the ragged bark, he was up in two minutes to the nest. He pulled the whole nest to pieces in a moment, and scattered the pieces over the rocks. The long feathers, which the boy was after, went flying about the ground.

Then he slipped back easily to the great knot where he had fastened the rope, and we called out to him to stop there a while. We had hoped that the bird would come back so that we could get a shot at her. Russell was surprised when he found we had been sitting up there on the ledge laughing at him all the time. But the old eagle would not come back, and probably thought a deserted home was not worth fighting about. I believe Russell afterwards caught her in a trap, at any rate he kept those eagle's feathers many years, which he took so much risk to get from the nest.

I have never forgotten that incident, not only because the boy was so persistent and ingenius, but because it was so unusual a thing for an eagle to be found in the mountains at that time of the year. His uncle said "No one on earth but Russell would have thought of such a thing, or ventured to climb for such a prize."

CHAPTER II.

BOYHOOD.

*Brother and sister—His boyhood's home—Father's occu-
pation—Hardships—School life—Daily work—Love
of animals—Sports—Saving lives—Love of storms—
An author's description of his old home.*

R USSELL H. CONWELL was the second son in
a family, with one brother and one sister. The
sister, now Mrs. Lyman T. Ring of Huntington,
Mass., is three years younger than Russell. His brother
Charles was in the United States service for a number
of years, during and after the war of the rebellion. He
died in 1871, having been for sometime attached to the
United States Survey of the Mississippi River, under
General Warren, U. S. A. Both his parents died soon
after, and all are buried in the Cemetery at Ringville,
in his native town of Worthington. The white slabs
which mark their graves can be seen a long distance
away, as the burial place is on a prominent little plateau
of those elevated highlands.

Russell's home was a very humble one, and his fare
of the most simple kind, as his parents began life

together very poor, and were obliged to save every penny to meet the interest on the farm. It would seem absurd, I suppose, to the farmers of the rich valleys, or on the western prairies, to give the name of "a farm" to such a collection of broken rocks, ledges, cliffs, sand heaps, brush clumps, muck hollows and barren hillsides, as was included in that little homestead of a hundred acres.

Russell's father was unable to get a living off the farm alone, and so contracted to lay stone walls for farms and house cellars. Russell's father was a very powerful man physically, and was regarded among us as the strongest man of muscle in the neighborhood. But he was also a man of unusual native talent, and soon saw that there was more money in the mercantile life than in stone masonry. So while Russell was a small boy his father began to gather up butter, eggs, cattle, sheep, wild animal's skins and various merchantable productions of the mountain towns, and periodically visited the city of Springfield, Mass., to dispose of them at a profit.

He was a man of unimpeachable moral character, and was respected and trusted implicitly by all who had dealings with him. Hence he did not need much money on which to transact business. He did not succeed in getting rich, but he did pay off the debt on his farm, and always gave liberally toward the church, schools and charitable enterprises. I never heard how much he had accumulated when he died, but he could not have been at any time worth over two thousand dollars. But he was a genial, good neighbor, and a consistent, active member of the Methodist Episcopal Church in the small hamlet of South Worthington.

Russell's early life must have been spent in the hardships of that struggle for a living. He was, at three years of age, sent to a district school two miles away, and the hilly path led over wild scenes and through deep woods. I have often heard him speak with tenderness of that dear old red school-house of his earliest recollections. But he could go to school only in the autumn or winter months, as he was needed on the farm to watch the sheep, or drive the cattle, or stable the horse, or chop the wood. His life began with work, and has been one of continuous employment.

His school life, as far as I can learn, from his school-mates, was not in any way remarkable, unless it be for the irresistible and provoking way he had of arousing mirth and making even the teacher laugh at his original ways and speeches. He early acquired a most wonderful power of memorizing which strangely enabled him to look at pages and afterwards study them before his mind's eye without the book. He was a special favorite during several terms, from a habit he had of bringing his pockets full of large sheepnose apples and generously giving them all away. I do not think he ate a single

THE CHURCH AT SOUTH WORTHINGTON.

apple himself for the weeks in which he came loaded. He was strong and rugged as the rocks, and he could do without his meals most sturdily, and give his dinner away to other school children. The old schoolhouse was a rude structure, and had rough benches and rough desks, with a large stove for burning logs of wood, in the center of the room. It is still standing, and is often pointed out to travelers on the Worthington stage which passes the house.

At home Russell and his brother slept in the attic under the roof, with the unpainted rafters and shingles over them, and the stormy winds moaning under the eaves, and sometimes rifts of snow drifting into the place through the cracks. His clothing was of cheap material, and often patched and ragged, as the most diligent mother could not keep such a boy in whole apparel. His daily tasks in early boyhood during the winter were a changeable, conflicting hurry, from building the morning fire before daylight to milking the cows, feeding the horse, cutting wood, caring for the sheep and pigs, shoveling out snow-drifts, mending ox-sleds, hunting for hen's eggs, peeling apples and general housework. If he went to school he or his brother, or both had to come home early or at noontime to care for the stock.

But his brother told me that Russell was the only one about the farm who was able to catch a wild cat, or could control the vicious cattle. He seemed to under-

stand them and they understood him. He would ride
down to the watering-place in the valley on a shy cow's
back, and come rushing back, holding with both arms
about the neck of a prancing ox. The calves would
kick up and chase him about among the rocks with a
childish delight. The wild squirrels and woodchucks
he often fed, and he was repeatedly overheard pronounc-
ing a funeral oration over some animal which others
had killed.

In summer time his boyish life was spent in shepherd
occupations, or in planting, hoeing or gathering the
scanty crops of corn, potatoes, beans and pumpkins
which constituted the entire harvest. He loved fruit
trees and planted them wherever there was hope of soil
between the stones to support them. One of the finest
apple orchards on the mountains is one which is still
wonderfully fruitful, and which he set out with young
trees, and grafted before he left the old homestead.
The broken hillsides, which he helped to clear of lum-
ber, are many of them overgrown again, and some of the
corn-fields where he attacked the weeds and pronounced
oratorical maledictions on them, as he worked on for
hours alone, are now covered with wild growths of
mountain blackberries and raspberries, and the fox,
woodchuck, muskrat, wild partridge and bluejay revel
in a wilderness there. But the barren hill-top behind
the old house, with a side growth of sugar-maple trees,

still remains unchanged. The old sugar-house in the forest, where he used to gather the maple sap in the spring, and where, through long nights he fed the chaldron fire, and read borrowed books by the flickering light, is still standing, I think. He cared but little for hunting, but took the prize in four or five contests at shooting matches, and has received several prizes at city matches since. But he enjoyed picking wild berries, and long expeditions into the woods, or nights and days of fishing at the ponds or lakes which fill so many of our mountain crests. Every lurking-place for trout in all the cascades, pools and eddies of the stream about the neighborhood, he was familiar with. But how he managed to get any time for such things, was ever a surprise. But he must have played truant sometimes, and the way he could write his father's name when skating one day on the mill-pond at the village, led his father to say, "Such things as that are not done without practice, and I guess I'll set him at peeling bark in the new clearing."

He was a powerful swimmer, and could get none of the boys to race with him in that sport. I heard of several cases where he saved persons from drowning by his skill as a swimmer. In one case, at Norwich Pond, he swam over a mile to an upset boat, and dove three times, bringing up a man and a boy who had gone down a second time. He had a gift for inventing, or improving fishing apparatus, oars, boats, coasting sleighs, household and farm utensils, and all sorts of wind and water toys.   He loved such pastimes, and his father often punished him with the rod for his persistence in their construction.   The only time his father ever asked his pardon, I have heard, was after he had whipped Russell for leaving the cider apples out in the frost while he worked on an improved ox-sled, which, afterward, was of great practical use.

The fierce winter storms, which in these mountains and this climate are often long and wild, were to Russell a delight.   He was out in the coldest weather, and driving snow-storms were no hindrance to his lonely excursions.   Often covered with icy sleet and sliding on snowdrifts deeper than his length, he found his way to the woods, or to school, or to the pickerel holes on the ponds without fear or complaint.   He was often the first thought of a neighbor, and always the first volunteer, when a sheep or calf had been lost in the hills or forests, and one of his older neighbors tells me that he remembers one night in a rocky pasture, two miles away from any house where at dawn he found a neighbor's lost cow nearly buried in the snow of the sudden storm.   His love for coasting on the icy crust in winter, when a smooth slab or two barrel staves served as a sleigh, was a positive passion.   The steepest side hills, and the many dangerous declivities and leaps were his attraction; and like an arrow he would dart down from peak to valley with a recklessness of manner that led all the old ladies to prophesy that "Russell will get killed one of these days."

But there seemed to be a skill back of all the venturesomeness which brought him safe at the foot of the hills. In summer he was out in the darkest thunder-showers, and seemed to have a strange pleasure in getting wet through, and in witnessing the near play of the lightning. A thunder-storm in the mountains was his great sport, and his mother told me that all the years of his boyhood, as soon as he heard the patter of the great drops on the shingles over his bed, or as soon as awakened by the distant thunder, he would always get up and sit at the open window, or go out into the night to watch the storm alone. Whether or not he cares for such things now, I do not know.

The attractive author Miss May Field McKean once visited the Conwell homestead, and published a description of her journey which contained the following:

"Just at present many thoughts are turning with interest toward the Green Mountains of Massachusetts, because in so doing they follow Russell H. Conwell to the home of his boyhood. But though fancy may have painted those scenes to which he has from time to time referred, during his public ministrations, or private utterances among us, yet to most of us the fancy is vague and undefined ; therefore we are sure we can lay before our readers nothing that can give them more pleasure than a description of that early home.

" Huntington Station, in Hampshire County, Mass., is twenty-one miles northwest of Springfield, on the Boston and Albany Railroad.   The residence of his sister and brother-in-law, Mr. and Mrs. Lyman T. Ring, is reached by a five-mile drive from here.   It is situated on the East Branch of the Westfield River, upon a sufficient eminence to command a fine view of the rapid river, and the surrounding country.

" But to reach the old homestead, one must drive six miles up the valley to South Worthington.   The course lay for a time along the river, and then followed a tributary to it, so that one did not once leave the sweet sound of falling water—for these swift mountain streams present but little likeness to the slow, dignified advance of our level-country rivers.   In fact they remind one very much of ' How the water comes down at Lodore.' "

> " ' From its fountains
>   In the mountains,
>   Through moss and through brake
>   It runs and it creeps
>   For a while, till it sleeps
>   In it's own little lake.
>   And thence at departing,
>   Awakening and starting,
>   It runs through the reeds,
>   And away it proceeds,

Through meadow and glade,
In sun and in shade—
Here it comes sparkling,
And there it lies darkling.

*   *   *   *   *

And so never ending, but always descending,
Sounds and motions forever are blending,' etc.

"And while this harmony of 'sounds and motions' was upon one side of the road, upon the other rose the mountains in some places almost perpendicularly, sometimes to considerable heights, thickly wooded with many kinds of trees, among the rocks at whose feet, fern and moss and shrub vied with each other in delicacy of shade and gracefulness of form and variety of beauty and bloom.

"Presently we were told : 'When we have passed the next bend in the road we can see the old church.' A few rods more, and high before us we saw the white gleam through the trees, seeming to give strength and calmness to the scene by its heavenward-pointing spire. Before reaching it we came to one of the wildest and most beautiful series of cascades that can be imagined.

"A particular characteristic of all these New England houses is the absolute neatness in which they are kept. Buildings which looked as if the contractors had finished their work this year, and the painters yesterday, were pointed out as having stood in the same neat order for half a century. The exterior of this church was no exception to the rule, though the interior showed the mistake. The Conwell pew was the second from the front on the right hand side—straight-backed, narrow-seated and square-armed. The gallery, where as a young man Mr. Conwell used to lead the singing, ran across the front of the church.

" From the window in this gallery the scene is exceedingly beautiful, commanding a view for many miles down the valley. Up to this time the weather had been threatening rain. Now the sun shone forth in splendor, but from a sky so full of clouds that they were constantly changing and completing the picture by their own beautiful forms and tints above, and their shadows on the valley and mountain sides below.

" A little beyond the church is the old homestead. The house, which stands upon a commanding eminence, is out of repair now, for it has gone into strangers' hands. Roses and running vines have been trained around the door once, but to-day they are neglected and forlorn-looking; weeds grow side by side with the lilies of former care, and the pathway has been encroached upon by the grass and shrubs of the door-yard.

" The view from the porch here is but little changed from that already noted at the church, and among the first sounds which greeted the infant ears of the children of the household must have been the 'music of the waters from the cascades below. Above the porch is the small-paned window into the attic which Mr. Conwell occupied when a boy, where he

> " Listened to the strain
> That was played upon the shingles
> By the patter of the rain."

" Back of the house is the old barn ; then a field that was a ball ground of years ago ; and then still farther ascending the brow of the mountain, capped by a huge rock from which the eye may turn in any direction and still behold a feast of beauty. The reader will not wonder that the writer gathered a piece of moss from the foot of this rock to be preserved as a souvenir of the spot. Again in fancy do we breathe long, sweet draughts of the pure mountain air, listen to the restless, ceaseless murmur of the now distant water, hear the melody of the birds' song and insect life, and note the perfect harmony of field and wood, of mountain and valley, of sunlight and shadow. 'Tis only in the sin- fulness of human life that we discover discord and incompleteness.

"Coming back we passed into the orchard. These trees were planted by Mr. Conwell himself. We had seen many trees heavily laden with fruit, but none so heavily as these. Although many of the branches were propped up, they still bowed low under their weight of promising fruitage, and we could not help asking the question whether there was not in this fact a prophecy that is being realized in the life of him who planted them.

"In a farther drive we were shown the schoolhouse where in youthful days he went to school, the spring where all the children drank on their way to and from thence, the building where he taught his first school, and the town hall where the people assembled from miles around to do honor to the returned soldiers, as described in the lecture 'Acres of Diamonds.' From this point—the table-land of the lower Green Mountains—can be seen the mountain near the birthplace and early home of William Cullen Bryant, who among this Hampshire County scenery, wrote his immortal 'Thanatopsis.'

"We once heard Dr. Henson say: 'It is the country boy whose eyes from childhood have looked off to grand distances, and whose strength has come from nearness to nature in her sublimity and beauty, who has a far-reaching mental vision, and who proves the greatest power in the world.' 'Well, we don't wonder.'"

CHAPTER III.

THE SCHOLAR.

His school days—Mental peculiarities—His teachers—Rev. Asa Niles—Industrious study—Books in his pockets — Wilbraham Academy—Cooking his mush alone—a poor boy at Yale—Kindness of professors—His first literary ventures—Interrupted studies—The war.

IN securing the information about Mr. Conwell's studies, and education generally, I have asked several of his highly-educated acquaintances to send me information, and this report is made up largely of their answers.

Russell was a rather dull scholar when a child, according to some of his teachers, and very troublesome sometimes in his rollicking mischievousness. But beginning at three years of age to go two miles over the hill-tops to school would seem like precociousness to me. But his teachers and books were not of the first order, and the ideas concerning teaching in a Yankee school district then and now, are quite different. He was often at the foot of his class, except when he was in a

branch by himself.   Yet he seemed to understand the
books, and in a curious, general way obtained knowledge speedily.   He once told me when he visited his
native town, to give a centennial address I think, that
there was one teacher, a Miss Salina Cole, afterward
Mrs. Parsons, to whom he was more indebted for his
education than to any other teacher or professor he ever
had.   She had some theory in psychology, or mind development, which she tried to use with the smaller
scholars, but which was a failure with nearly every one
but Russell.   She tried to train them to remember by
a kind of pholographic process in the mind, which I
could not easily explain.   It was a hobby, or fancy of
the time or place.   By it the children were supposed
to be able to repeat long recitations verbatim, by reading them over but once.   It was done by scrutinizing
the page closely, and word by word, once, and then
shutting the eyes and reproducing the actual page on
the mind so as to read it off, word for word.   It has
really been a wonder in his case.   He could repeat
many pages without an error, even in the punctuation.
But he could not do it with his eyes open.   He seemed
to actually see the page in his mind.   He said that some
of those pages he recited then, came to him twenty-
five years after, when in certain conditions of mental
excitement, and every word is as clear as the print.
Under favorable, but often curious conditions, he can

now read once a whole chapter of the Bible, and recite the whole of it hours after without having attempted to "commit it to memory" on the plan of "learning by heart."

But the ablest teacher of his early years, and the person who encouraged him to aspire to scholarship, was the Rev. Asa Niles, a local Methodist preacher, and father of Prof. W. H. Niles of Cambridge, Mass. The Rev. Asa Niles was a noble character, and as a teacher he was strict and energetic. Russell and his brother Charles were inspired by that good man to seek a higher education. Mr. Niles was a cousin of Russell's fa·her, and the relationship may have increased the interest. The three boys, Russell and Charles and William H. Niles were the closest of friends, and loved the same studies.

Prof. W. H. Niles is now one of the most honored professors at the Technological Institute at Boston, Mass., and is well known as a scientific lecturer throughout the country. Rev. Asa Niles watched over Russell almost as over his own son, and while often provoked by Russell's wildness, yet clung to him nobly. He it was who had influence enough with Russell's father to obtain permission for the boy to go to Wilbraham Academy, after the local schools were exhausted in his line of studies. It was he that encouraged Russell to teach school at sixteen years of age, and as Russell's

father was poor, it was a sacrifice for him to give up the
boy's wages just as he could earn something. But Mr.
Niles was respected by all, and an especial friend of
Russell's father, because of their membership in the
little M. E. Church at the head of the valley. Russell
obtained about all the privileges Mr. Niles asked.

It was Mr. Niles who suggested to Russell the course
he has always pursued, and which has made him such
a scholar. Mr. Niles advised him to take a book with
him at all times, and study every spare moment, wherever he might be. Russell adopted it heartily. In the
hayfield, at noon hour, or in the potato patch at the end
of each row he would glance at the book and meditate
on the page as he continued his work. When driving
an ox-team to the distant railroad, or when using the
horse on the road or in the fields and forest, wherever
there was a short or long drive, Russell produced his
worn book and learned something. Even his father,
who was a man of excellent judgment, made jokes
about Russell's bookishness. But the boy stuck to it,
and I think carries books about with him still in the
busy life of to-day.

When Russell was sixteen years old he went to the
Academy at Wilbraham, at the edge of the Connecticut
Valley, twelve miles east of Springfield, Mass. He
was too poor to go but one term at a time, in company
with his brother, and even then they earned their board

by working after study hours for the farmers about the village. I was told while in the army, by one of his classmates, that during one term Russell had a room on the outskirts of the village and lived alone, and his entire food for several weeks was Indian mush and milk prepared by himself.

Such a broken life interrupted his studies much, so that he never stood very high in his classes. His studies and reading, however, took a wide range, and he mastered many books not in the curriculum of studies. He was independent of criticism or standing in the Academy, made so, I suppose, by his hardships and inability to dress as well as the more favored students. But there he met with a sympathetic friend and helper in the Rev. Miner Raymond, D. D., principal of the Academy, and made many friends among a class of men, many of whom are now high in the world's success.

For three years, 1859, 1860, and 1861, Russell labored a part of the time at the Academy, a part of the time teaching school in Blandford, Mass., or at West Granville (Beach Hill), Mass., and a part of the time helping his father on the farm.

In 1861 and the first part of 1862 Russell went to Yale College with his brother Charles. There he was too poor to enter on the regular classical course in the college, but met with a most generous reception from sympathetic professors.

He had decided to study for the law, although all the time inclined toward the ministry. He found that he could save time and money by working hard and taking the law and classics together. The privations he endured, and the hard work he performed soon threw him into a dangerous fever. But even on his bed he kept up his law studies, and held through to the examination in the Law School. Prof. Silliman and the president of the college urged him to take less work, and offered to assist him with money, but he declined to borrow money. It was a generous, and most creditable kindness, which led those professors to give extra time from their private hours to help on that poor boy so that he might be able to enter the junior year by examination.

Such men are an honor to our colleges. Yet when we think how at that sensitive age those young brothers faced the ridicule of students in wealth, and struggled against such great obstacles to obtain an education, we can account readily for the consequent success. Charles selected at Yale a scientific pursuit, and Russell chose the law.

Something of the genius of the boy at the beginning of his study at New Haven is seen in a poem, quite extensively copied then, which he wrote for the North-ampton Gazette, but which I obtained from the Somerville Journal, published by Mr. Conwell's brother-in-law J. O. Hayden. The first verse is all I need copy:

" There's a time in the night
When an editor's light
Burns in his sanctum dimly.
When his eye is fired,
And his tongue inspired
With thought and reason seemly.
Oh, oh could he pen
The thoughts that come then,
And fill his room so lonely,
'Twould build him a name
'Mid the temples of fame,
Compared with the greatest only.'

But into the feverish rush and exhausting toil of that student's life came the patriotic call. His country needed men to maintain the supremacy of freedom. and he suddenly broke away. Both he and his brother determined one evening to leave all and go to war. Russell attempted to enlist as a private in the 27th Massachusetts Infantry, and signed the papers, but his father's objection prevented the mustering officer from accepting him.

But when the 46th Massachusetts Infantry was called out, the unanimous and urgent demand of Company F for him as captain, led Governor Andrew to commission the beardless boy.

But he went on with his studies. Books, books everywhere! Study, study at all times when off duty. Often I saw him wandering off up the banks of the Neuse River at New Berne, N. C., or out into the cotton fields,

or in his tent studying Blackstone or Greenleaf.   After
our term of service was over, and he had entered the
artillery service, he continued his persistent study.   At
Fort Macon, N. C., when in command of the outposts,
he walked up and down the shore, and learned by heart
chapter after chapter of law and philosophy.   His in-
dependence and almost recklessness as a soldier, which
continually got him into trouble, did not abate his
studiousness.

After his wounds at Kennesaw Mountain, Ga., and
return to Massachusetts, he entered the law office
of Judge W. S. Shurtleff of Springfield, his former
Colonel, and from there went to the University of
Albany, N. Y., where he graduated on examination.
The Albany University conferred on him the degree of
LL. B.   But his education was but partially begun.   For
all the years of law practice, of foreign travel, of editorial
and ministerial life, he has ever been at his books.   He
learned to read five different languages in the daily
rides on the steam and horse cars, between his home in
Newton Centre, Mass., and his office in Boston.

Some of the most difficult sciences he mastered alone
on steam cars, or in stage coaches, while journeying as
a correspondent in distant countries, or in distant
American states.   A professor at Oberlin College has
preserved as a curiosity, an autograph book which was
handed to Mr. Conwell at the Paris Exhibition of 1878,

and in which Mr. Conwell wrote impromptu three
verses of "Mary had a little lamb," in seven different
languages.

[His establishment of the Temple College, Philadelphia, for workingmen, is said to have grown out of the
desire of a class of young men, to get directions from
him, how to study at home and during spare hours.—
ED.]

He tried to learn something of every man he met,
and from every new thing he saw.

He did not appear to be systematic, but persistent.
His motto written in autograph books, but more clearly
written in his character, is *Perseverentia Vincit*, "Perseverance Conquers." Surely his life proves the old
proverb to be true.

When he began his theological studies, I do not
know, but it was many years before he entered the ministry, for I remember being told by his father as early
as 1867 that Russell was collecting a theological library,
and sending to Germany for a number of books on the
subject, which were delayed in the Boston Custom
House. In 1865 when he was admitted to the bar in
the Supreme Court of New York, he is said to have
had a Greek New Testament in his overcoat pocket.
The same evening when he was admitted in 1875 to
practice in the United States Supreme Court at Washington, he delivered an address in that city on the

branches taught in the old school of the prophets.   He
was regarded as a scholar in theology, and gathered
about him in Boston several hundred students who
wished to listen to his exposition of the scriptures, before he intended to enter the ministry.   Living at Newton Centre, Mass., the seat of a celebrated theological
seminary of the Baptist denomination, he was brought
into intimate relations with some of the best minds, and
with some of the profoundest biblical scholars.   His
chief interest for some years centered in Christian an-
tiquities.   He gathered from all parts of the old world
photographs of the ancient manuscripts, and of sacred
places, and kept up a frequent correspondence with
many professors and explorers interested in that subject.   He often lectured in schools and colleges on
Archæological subjects, with illustrations prepared for
the calcium light under his own supervision.   When
his library was destroyed by fire, the greatest loss
was in valuable theological works.   His theological
course at the Newton Theological Seminary was wholly
elective, and maintained together with a multitude of
active business and pastoral duties.   He is a man who
always finds work enough to do, and cannot be said to
be ever idle.   He left the Newton Institution in 1881
when he gave himself wholly to the ministerial office.

CHAPTER IV.

THE ORATOR.

Speaking at eight years of age—Organizer of a debating society at twelve—A natural musician—Ambition to be an actor—His nervousness when expecting to speak —Address in Whitman Hall, Westfield—Address in Leeds, England—Removal to Minnesota—The failure of his health—Opening a law office at Boston—Forced to the platform in political campaigns—No apparent effort at oratorical effect—His celebrated lecture delivered one thousand times.

FOR some years I preserved the newspapers and pamphlets containing Mr. Conwell's speeches. But the number grew so fast that I gave up the idea. But I need not copy them, as probably nearly all my comrades are acquainted with those which most interested me.

Russell was always an orator. He was born so. His mother said that before he could speak plainly he was constantly delivering imaginary sermons to the cat or pigs. And one day when he was but six years old, she overheard him delivering an oration to the astonished rooster on the fence. He was brought out on all occasions, and was a necessity to the school exhibitions and anniversaries. Often whenever he was left alone he would begin addressing an unseen audience, and blushed to the ears when suddenly overheard. He talked to the trees, to the corn stalks, to the potato tops, and anathematized the weeds before he cut them down.

When he was but eight years of age, during a time of local excitement over some question concerning Spiritualism, a crowded audience gathered in the Methodist Church to listen to his address. He was not more than twelve years of age when he was the foremost organizer of a debating society which met every week in the district school-house.

There with grown men he held his own in debate, and was listened to with surprise and respect. The green, awkward country boy, with torn hat and patched knees, was talked about up and down the valleys. Fortunately for the boy, his parents had the good sense to avoid praising him. Sometimes his father gave him severe whippings for his literary lampoons.

He was a natural musician, and easily mastered any instrument, and as a boy, was esteemed by us country people as a good singer.

For some years he was the chief reliance as a player, on whatever instrument was handiest for the dance, at young peoples parties and balls. At the time he taught school he was also an excellent music teacher, and many of his scholars are still living, and playing or singing. But he often composed both words and music to songs having local hits, and often sharply sarcastic. Any local gossip, or practical joke awoke his muse, and a fearful raking some of the people received in song. It was for these dreaded ballads that Russell's father often used the birch stick. But it did no good. The very next night some original song, which hurt unintentionally, some old lady's feelings, would convulse the listeners as he sat at the parlor organ, or drew the bow of the violin. It was the cause of many heartburnings.

A good story about him appeared in the Philadelphia papers in 1883 which shows that the early traits are not extinct. He still has the faculty of composing words and music, and uses it often in his church work. He was engaged in writing out something of the kind that summer day, on the great pier at Cape May, N. J. A band from New York were on the pier practicing for their evening playing, and the cornetist went fishing. The cornet lay on a seat near Mr. Conwell and he took it up and played from his notes to try his composition. Then suddenly recalling an old air, he broke out into a solo that attracted the attention of all the people about the pier. He then laid down the instrument and walked away. About an hour later one of the band,

not knowing who Mr. Conwell was, accosted him at
his cottage gate and offered him five dollars, and then
ten dollars to play for him, as a substitute, in the ball
at Congress Hall.

These songs of his boyhood were often recited by
him on public occasions. But in those early days his
great ambition was to be an actor. His greatest delight
was in dialogues and theatrical performances. Alas,
the little country church up there on the hill-top has
seen many a theatrical play, on the improvised stage
built over its altar rail for a school exhibition. Old
saints laughed till they cried at Russell's acting, and
unintentionally encouraged him in his foolish ambition.

In some one of his lectures delivered years ago Mr.
Conwell related how he was cured of the mania, and
as near as I remember it was in this way.

One spring, during the maple sugar season, when he
was driving back and forth from the mountains to the
Huntington Station on the Boston and Albany Railroad,
carting maple sugar, he left the seat of his wagon at
home. On his way back he was compelled to drive the
horse and stand up in the rickety old wagon with no
support. It is a difficult thing to do in most favorable
circumstances. About five miles down in the deep
valley below his home was a very dense piece of wood-
land. The road which ran through it was a very lone-
some place. When entering that wood Russell drove

the old horse at a trot, and thought it would be a good place to practice his part in the next theatrical performance.

His chosen part was that of an insane person who rushed in to interrupt some love scene, by saying, "Woe! woe! unto you all, ye children of men!" So Russell stood up in the wagon behind the trotting horse holding the loose reins, and shouted out, "Woe! woe!" The obedient horse thought it was a most imperative command to stop. He did stop instantly. Over Russell went like an arrow. He fell upon the horse's back, and slid down head first upon the shaft, and sprawled out in four inches deep of spring mud. In falling he cut his forehead on the step fastened to the shaft, and the scar on his head is still plainly to be seen. It bled profusely, and his appearance in mud and blood caused his father to make fun of him so persistently that he was ashamed to appear in the piece. He never took part in such plays after that. He stooped to conquer.

Notwithstanding his love of public speaking, he was always as nervous as a child whenever expecting to speak in public. One of his classmates at Wilbraham, and a member with him of a debating society, there called "The Club," told me at the time when Mr. Conwell delivered the oration at the dedication of the soldiers' monument at Billerica, Mass., of the first time Russell as a boy appeared in a debate at the Wilbraham school. He had written out or thought out and committed to memory a long speech, and as usual with school boys, quoted Patrick Henry.

But all he could say in his confusion on being called up unexpectedly soon, was to stammer out, after many struggles and tears, "Give me liberty or give me death." The incident was published in the column of jokes in the Springfield Republican soon after, in 1859. But he soon became the leader in debate, and among many boys who have since become successful men, he took the foremost position as a speaker. Like John B. Gough, whom Mr. Conwell somewhat resembles, and who was many years his firm friend, Mr. Conwell has never wholly overcome that nervous sensitiveness when he is about to address an audience.

In the law schools Russell seldom appeared in the moot courts or debates. He was too poor to dress to his taste, and for that reason shunned all publicity. But when the war opened in 1861, although he was but seventeen years of age, he suddenly became famous in Western Massachusetts as a patriotic speaker.

It was a wonderful thing, and drew crowds of excited listeners wherever he went. Towns sent for him to help them raise their quotas of soldiers, and the ranks speedily filled before his inspiring and patriotic speeches. In 1862 I remember a scene at Whitman Hall in Westfield, Mass., which none who were there can forget.

Russell had delivered two addresses there before. On that night there were two addresses before his by prominent lawyers, but there was evident impatience to hear "The boy." When he came forward there was the most deafening applause. He really seemed inspired by miraculous powers. Every auditor was fascinated and held closely bound. There was for a time breathless suspense, and then at some telling sentence the whole building shook with wild applause. At its close a shower of bouquets from hundreds of ladies carpeted the stage in a moment, and men from all parts of the hall rushed forward to enlist. The keeper of the Park Hotel says that he had the bouquets brought from the hall in large clothes hampers. Mr. Conwell was the idol of the Westfield public for the time, and it is a wonder that the boy retained his senses. Every one said it would make him vain, and hinder his success, but still kept up their praise. During his service in the war he could not have had many opportunities to speak except in addressing meetings of soldiers which were seldom held. In 1863 or 1864 I think, when he re-enlisted after one term of service, he delivered his first lyceum lecture. Then he began that public career as a popular lecturer which has made him so well known in the United States and in England. His lecture that evening was on some historical subject, bearing on the benefits of previous wars, and was delivered for the students of Mt. Holyoke Seminary in Hadley, Mass.

I heard Mr. Conwell say some years ago that the lecture was a failure financially, and in delivery. Perhaps a failure then was the best thing that could happen to him, beginning so young. Many young heads have been turned to foolishness by early success.

But in the beginning of his public work as an orator there appeared the great influence of the musical training, and the most attractive thing about it perhaps, then, was the thoughts awakened and the impressions made by the musical changes and tones in his voice. When he delivered an address in Leeds, England, in 1870, on the "Old and New England," a critic writing for the London *Telegraph* said: "The young man is weirdly like his native hills. You can hear the cascades and the trickling streams in his tone of voice. He has a strange and unconscious power of so modulating his voice as to suggest the howl of the tempest in rocky declivities, or the soft echo of music in distant valleys. There would be great difference of opinion about his cleverness as a debater, but the breezy freshness and natural suggestiveness of varied nature in its wild state was completely fascinating. He excelled in description. and the auditor could almost hear the Niagara roll as he described it, and listened to catch the sound of sighing pines in his voice as he told of the

Carolinas. He was so unlike any other speaker, so completely natural that his blunders disarmed criticism."

After the war he went to Minnesota and stayed for a time at St. Paul, where he united with the First Baptist Church, and where he made many friends. Afterwards he moved to Minneapolis, and opened a law and real estate office in that marvellously growing city. I do not know much of his career there as a public speaker, although I have heard that he lectured through the state and took such an active part in political campaigns and temperance contests, as to make many friends and also some bitter enemies.

In his Fourth of July Oration in Springfield, Mass., 1875, he spoke of the happy days in Minnesota, and made that well remembered eulogy on Minnesota, that " Garner of America's noblest men and women."

After the failure of his health through the breaking out of wounds while running to the fire which destroyed his home, he was obliged to leave the platform for a time, and became an extensive traveler. But in the Southern States, in the Western States and Territories, in California, China ports, India and England he was often compelled to deliver addresses, and when his health returned, and he opened a law office at Boston, Mass., his regular work as a platform lyceum lecturer became an established profession. For fifteen years he has been well-known and eagerly sought for through-

out the New England and the Middle States. His lectures on science, literature, theology and travel, were
again and again repeated in the same cities and towns.
He was often forced to the platform in political campaigns.

During all this time he was continually addressing
Sunday-schools on special occasions, and for years
delivered lay sermons on Sunday evenings for missions
and destitute churches. It was as a lay preacher that
he began his work in Lexington, Mass., where he was
afterwards ordained. I have been told that the first
Sabbath he preached there he had but seventeen
auditors, but in a few weeks the house was crowded to
the street at every service.

When he removed to Philadelphia, he began again
with a small congregation of about one hundred, and
the triumphs which have followed were only to be expected by his old acquaintances. With a church so
crowded that public safety compelled the use of tickets
of admission issued long in advance, and with a pros-
pective church soon to be completed which will seat in
the pews between four and five thousand people he
stands where all of us expected he would stand. As a
preacher he has the same fidelity to nature and is as
simple and as earnest as a child. There is said to be
no apparent effort at oratorical effect. He rises and
falls like our spring floods, and never wrote out a

sermon in his life for delivery. He is different from any other man. He can be compared with no one, yet not called eccentric. He speaks for some definite object. He gains it. In a few years his church in Philadelphia became one of the largest in the country, and as a pulpit orator he is now well known throughout the nation. Through what winding paths America's greatest men reach distinction ! Mr. Conwell's character and oratory is a constant reproduction of our New England mountains, cloud-capped, granite hills, magnificent landscapes, deep valleys, wild woods, cliffs, dashing streams and autumn grandeur, all appear in varying ways in Mr. Conwell's utterances. He is fitly named "The Picturesque Orator."

Mr. Conwell's celebrated lecture entitled "Acres of Diamonds," had been delivered nearly one thousand times in 1881, and that is but one of a long list, which he delivers in his winter tours, and at summer commencements and anniversaries. At Chautauqua his addresses draw crowded audiences, and when he lectured in the Mormon Tabernacle at Salt Lake City, on "Men of the Mountains," it is said that before the sale was stopped, over twelve thousand purchased tickets to hear him on one evening. His correspondence, answering applications for addresses, lectures and sermons, reach often a hundred letters a day.

CHAPTER V.

THE AUTHOR.

He edits the Minneapolis Chronicle—He writes for the Boston Traveller—He is engaged as a regular correspondent for London and New York papers—His first book, "Why and how the Chinese emigrate"—Memorial services of Bayard Taylor—Longfellow's poem—List of Mr. Conwell's books.

I AM not altogether sure that I have seen all of Mr. Conwell's books, and I must often refer to the opinion of others. His descriptive powers as a writer were first exhibited in his correspondence for newspapers. He became first known in connection with his own paper, the Minneapolis *Chronicle*, which was afterwards merged with the *Atlas* into the Minneapolis *Tribune*. But later, when he wrote a remarkable series of letters for the Boston *Traveller*, his success became permanent. He visited all the battle fields of the Civil War in the Southern States and described their appearance five years after the war. The letters were copied throughout the country, and "Russell's Letters from the Battle Fields" were regularly seen in all parts of the land, copied from the *Traveller* entire. He identified many graves and many skeletons, and corrected many historical errors.

He gathered a large collection of mementoes from the battle fields, which people in the North and the South recognized as belonging to their friends and loved ones. His descriptions were so vivid that old soldiers would exclaim as they read, "That's where I stood," or, "I can see the whole battle again." Those letters called attention to him in other places, and he was soon engaged as a regular correspondent for London and New York papers. His letter from Hong Kong, China, to the New York *Tribune* on "Chinese Emigration" innocently caused some diplomatic difficulty through the exposure of the labor contract system.

One of his letters to the Boston *Traveller* in 1870 contained the widely known account of the gambling-house and the reforming influence of Miss Carey's hymn :

> "One sweetly solemn thought
> Comes to me o'er and o'er,
> I'm nearer my home to-day
> Than I've ever been before."

The story is published in full in "Butterfield's Story of the Hymns," and in "Long's History of Hymns," and in many other books. The reform of the rough old sailor by hearing his young companion sing those words carelessly has had an indirect influence in saving many young men from crime.

Mr. Conwell's description of the Himalaya Moun-tains, a magazine article published in 1872, was care-fully preserved by Henry Ward Beecher, and quoted by him in an address in New Hampshire in 1879. When Mr. Conwell returned home in 1871 from a tour entirely around the world, Lee & Shepard of Boston published his first book, entitled, "Why and How the Chinese Emigrate." The book had a large sale in this country owing to the fame of Mr. Conwell's letters and the excitement over Chinese emigration. But the book was nearly spoiled by the artist who illustrated it in a manner almost grotesque. The book is out of print now.

Soon afterwards a Boston firm published a volume written by him on "Woman and the Law." The book contained a collection of facts and legal decisions, and a discussion of the rights women had under the law which men did not enjoy. It caused a heated debate in the Massachusetts Legislature. The woman suffragists were at first incensed at the author. I will not say much about it lest I awaken a subject that Mr. Conwell may be glad is dead. No one tried to refute his data, however.

After that several volumes were published, and among them "The History of the Great Fire in Boston," "The History of the Great Fire in St. John," "The Life of Rutherford B. Hayes," and "The Life of James A.

Garfield." Mr. Conwell had been a traveling companion of Bayard Taylor, the great traveler, and was in intimate correspondence with Mr. Taylor the year of his death, while minister to Germany. At the memorial services held at Tremont Temple, Boston, Mr. Conwell was called upon to preside, and the suggestions of that great tribute to Mr. Taylor led Mr. Conwell to write a book upon Mr. Taylor's life. In a volume of Mr. Conwell's sermons I have found the following reference to that memorial occasion :

"When Bayard Taylor, the traveler and poet, died, great sorrow was felt and exhibited by the people of this nation. I remember well the sadness that was noticed in the city of Boston. The spontaneous desire to give some expression to the respect in which Mr. Taylor's name was held, pressed the literary people of Boston, both writers and readers, forward to a public memorial gathering. That audience of the scholarly classes was a wonderful tribute to a remarkable man, and one for which I feel still a keen sense of gratitude. I remember asking Mr. Longfellow to write a poem and to read it ; and, standing on the broad step at his front door in Cambridge, he replied to my suggestion with the sweet expression, 'The universal sorrow is almost too sacred to touch with a pen.'

"But when the evening came, although Professor Longfellow was too ill to be present, his poem was there. The great hall was crowded with the most cultivated people of Boston. On the platform sat many of the poets, orators and philosophers who have since passed into the beyond. When, after several speeches had been made, I arose to introduce Dr. Oliver Wendell Holmes, the pressure of the crowd was too great for me to reach my chair again, and I took for a time the seat which Dr. Holmes had just left, and next to Ralph Waldo Emerson. Never were words of poet listened to with a silence more respectfully profound than were the words of Professor Longfellow's poem as they were so touchingly and beautifully read by Dr. Holmes.

> ' Dead he lay among his books,
> The peace of God was in his looks!
> * * * * *
> Let the lifeless body rest,
> He is gone who was its guest,—
> Gone as travelers haste to leave
> An inn, nor tarry until eve!
> Traveler, in what realms afar,
> In what planet, in what star,
> In what vast aerial space,
> Shines the light upon thy face?
> In what gardens of delight
> Rest thy weary feet to-night? '
> * * * * *

Before Dr. Holmes resumed his seat, Mr. Emerson whispered in my ear, in his epigrammatic style, ' This is holy Sabbath time.' "

The " Life of Bayard Taylor " was hastily written for
a subscription sale. It had no marked literary merit,
but reached a great sale through agents. That volume
was followed by an enlarged edition of John S. C.
Abbott's "Lives of the Presidents," published by E. C.
Allen, of Augusta, Me. Mr. Conwell was a friend of
Mr. Abbott, and was a fitting person to bring up the
history to the present time. That book is still greatly
in demand. During the political campaign of 1880
Mr. Conwell's publishers brought out a " Life of James
G. Blaine," which was very popular, but too hastily
prepared to have a long demand.

Since his residence in Philadelphia the Baptist Publication Society have issued a volume written by him
on " Joshua Gianavello." It is a sketchy biography of
that great Waldensian chieftain, and vividly portrays
the manners and heroism of those terrible days of
religious persecution.

[Since the above was written the Miller Magee Co.
of Philadelphia have published a large volume by his
pen, with the title of " Acres of Diamonds." It is
written on the same plan and with the same funda-
mental ideas as his popular lecture of the same name.
It gives direction and encouragement to a worthy ambition to become great or honestly wealthy. It will
live in the market beyond this generation.]

CHAPTER VI.

THE SOLDIER.

Drilling the schoolboys—Not permitted to enlist on account of his age—Studied military tactics for the sake of knowing—Elected captain by unanimous vote—His enthusiastic and patriotic address—Oration delivered in Springfield—He is presented with a costly sword—Battle at Kingston—Battle at Goldsboro—The march through the swamp—A night attack—Bravery of Orderly Spencer—Caring for his soldiers—Reckless disregard of army orders—The battle at Newport Barracks—Brave Johnny Ring—Saving the captain's sword—Persecution—Promotion—In the western army—Wounded at Kennesaw—Leaving the service—Suffering from wounds.

TO his comrades I am sure this record will be a welcome message, for the call for some memorial account has been most imperative. The young soldier whom we learned to admire, and many of us to deeply love, may be too far up in the ascents of fame and greatness to be affected by it. It is a

SCALING THE EAGLE'S NEST. 55

simple tribute at the best, and from one little acquainted with such writing. But a soldier's heart beats
in sincere friendship, and that is the motive for writing these pages. It is but a few months since I
saw an old wooden sword which had been lying
about the old Conwell homestead ever since Russell
was ten years old. He made it out of a board, and
paraded up and down the barnyard with it, giving
orders to his troops of calves, sheep and poultry. He
saw a Fourth of July parade at Springfield, Mass.,
in his boyhood, and ever after kept organizing the
school boys into military companies. There was one
company bearing the strange name of "Silence" organized and decorated with badges by him. Mr.
Austin Hancock of Huntington, Mass., one of our
best loved comrades, still recalls the contract for the
badges.

Russell was but a boy when the war broke out, and
it seems now so strange that old men would have been
willing to be led into battle under the command of
such a country boy. But it was his fascinating eloquence which won him the hearts of all. If the war
had been ten years later Mr. Conwell would have worn
a star instead of a silver leaf. I well remember when
our regiment [the 46th Mass.] was being recruited how
absurd it seemed to us older men to think of his appointment as an officer, until we heard him speak. He

was mentioned by the men for lieutenant, for captain, for major and by a few for colonel, and I think he was only eighteen years old.

He had enlisted as a private in the 27th Massachusetts Regiment and was refused on account of his age. But when he enlisted as a private in the 46th the government needed men and was less particular about the age. The boy was in demand in several places as an officer, because he had improved his time at school and studied the tactics until he could order any maneuvers. It was just like him. He did not expect to command, but he took a book of military tactics in his pocket and studied the movements and orders just for the sake of knowing. So when the urgent call came from President Lincoln for "one hundred thousand more" he could drill a company or regiment like an old officer. I remember how the first time we assembled as a company, we were all completely astonished to find that boy perfectly at home in military tactics. We were proud of him. We wanted him for our captain. There was no rival. No one thought of canvassing for the office against him. He was elected captain by a unanimous vote. A committee was appointed to wait on Governor Andrew, to persuade him to commission Russell, and overcome the objection on account of his youth. Russell has always loved these mountains, but no better than we mountaineers have loved him. The company of which he was chosen captain was composed of men from Worthington, Plainfield, Chesterfield, Huntington, Chester, Middlefield, Russell and Blandford; those towns being the most rugged and mountainous in this part of the state. So the company was naturally called " The Mountain Boys," and went by that title ever afterwards. " The Boy Captain of the Mountain Boys " was often pointed out as a curiosity in the valley villages, after he had donned his first uniform. The rendezvous of the company was at Huntington, Mass. There a grand banquet was given to the soldiers before their departure for the war. At the table Russell made one of his enthusiastic and patriotic addresses, and so many men endeavored to enlist in the company after the limit was reached, that even Russell's own brother had to go with the overflow into another company.

In an oration delivered at the Opera House in Springfield, at the reunion of his regiment in 1873, Mr. Conwell referred with much feeling to that day. He said that war was at that time a hard, fierce fact, and men who enlisted then knew it meant hardship and many probabilities of death. But they pressed into the service.

Oh, that first night in bivouac at Camp Banks in the Connecticut Valley, near Springfield! Hungry, cold. The ground for a bed, a spadeful of earth for a pillow.

It was a rough beginning of soldier life. Russell loaned his new military overcoat to a boy soldier by the name of Porter, and rolled himself in a tent cloth. But the regiment was composed of earnest business men from the valleys, and hardy farmers from the mountains, and hardships did not dampen their patriotism.

Colonel Bowler, a preacher from Westfield, was the commander. Colonel W. S. Shurtleff, who has since been one of the best judges Massachusetts has ever commissioned, was the lieutenant colonel. Colonel Walkley, of Westfield, was then major. Colonel Bowler's resignation soon after we reached North Carolina, led to the promotion of all, and brought Captain Spooner, since Mayor of Springfield, up to the rank of major. Our company was lettered F, and held that place in the line throughout that term of service.

No surviving comrade of the regiment can forget the day when the soldiers presented Captain Conwell with that costly sword. There was a stand erected in the camp, and Colonel Shurtleff, I think, made the speech of presentation. Captain Conwell's reply was surpassingly eloquent. The shining gold sheath glittered in the sun, and the decorated handle gleamed most brightly; but it was outshone by brilliant words. The deep hush and the following cheers were not to be forgotten. On the sword were inscribed these words of affection :

> Presented to Captain Russell H. Conwell by the soldiers of Company F, 46th Mass. Vol. Militia, known as "The Mountain Boys." *Vera Amicitia est sempiterna.* [True friendship is eternal.]

The subsequent sad history of the sword has made it a precious keepsake, and Mr. Conwell, I am told, keeps it hanging over his bed where he can look upon it every day.

The regiment, after breaking camp, went by train to Boston, where it was received by the Governor, and was quartered in Faneuil Hall, the "Cradle of Liberty."

The secret expedition with which our regiment was connected consisted of several other Massachusetts regiments, including the 44th and 45th. We embarked in Boston harbor just as a great equinoctial storm came on. The gale grew so wild that we could not get the steamer out to sea, and with much difficulty the whole body of troops was landed, to wait until the storm was passed. In the suffering and danger of that beginning of warlike experiences, Captain Conwell began to show the material of which he was made. His sympathy with the suffering men and the readiness with which he divided his allowance with his own men can never be forgotten.   I hear it mentioned at almost every reunion of the regiment.   But he paid little regard for the mere formalities of military life from the first.   If he wanted a thing, he went for it.   If one of his men needed help, Captain Conwell gave it without regard to military rules.   No captain was more implicitly obeyed, and no company took more pride in their drill and appearance on parade.   If the captain wished it so, it was all we wanted to know.   I do not think he ever understood how his soldiers loved him.   He was tireless in looking after them.   He must have given away the greater part of his salary in sutler stores for the sick, or to make the soldiers' quarters more comfortable.

After a stormy voyage and a fearfully sick one to many of the men who had never seen the sea before, we rounded Cape Hatteras, off the coast of North Carolina, and steamed up the Neuse River to Newbern, N. C.   General Burnside had already captured the town, and we were placed under command of Major General J. G. Foster, and attached to a brigade with the 25th and 27th Massachusetts, and the 3d and 5th Massachusetts.   General Horace C. Lee, colonel of the 27th, commanded the brigade.   After several weeks of camp and garrison duty, our companies were sent off in detachments on garrison duty, and four companies came into their first actual contest with the enemy at

Batchelor's Creek, about seven miles above Newbern. But the severest campaigning of that winter was in the "Goldsboro expedition." Almost the entire marching force of the army at that point was on that march into the interior. The purpose of the advance was to cut the Weldon Railroad at Goldsboro, N. C., in conjunction with a general advance to be made in Virginia. It was indeed a hard march, but with short and uncertain halts we pushed on, and with only occasional cavalry skirmishes, which left beside the road the first Confederates we had ever seen, we hurried on to Kingston, N. C., on the Neuse River. There came the first battle. It was in earnest. The enemy held the bridge, and intended to keep it, but the brave charge made by the 9th New Jersey and the 10th Connecticut secured the field. The woods and a little open field near an old negro church were covered with the dead and dying. What an awful sight! We were brought up to the support of a New York battery, and followed closely the retreating enemy. It was our first battle. It caused but little damage to our regiment, but it brought us into the scenes of carnage which I suppose no soldier feels so keenly in after experience. The groans, the ghastly bodies, the streaming blood, the torn bodies! Alas for war!

That night we bivouacked in Kingston. I remember forgetting the scene of blood in chasing up and down a field after a small, black pig with two comrades, with a common intention of giving Captain Conwell a slice of fresh pork, cooked over a camp fire. We secured the pig. Captain Conwell had a large slice, but it may be that he gave it away.

When the troops reached the Weldon Railroad at the bridge below Goldsboro, another battle was fought. There the enemy had amassed a large body of troops to save their lines of communication and supplies. The artillery battle was terrific, and the enemy repeatedly charged our line. I recall the time when a long line of gray appeared approaching us through the fields. We were ordered to lie down, so that the shot and shell would pass over us. Our batteries were on a knoll a few rods in advance of our lines, and the noise of bursting shell was hideous. Captain Conwell walked forward up to the guns, and stood there in the smoke, exposed to the fire of the enemy, then close upon us. Many of us remonstrated with him for the useless risk he thoughtlessly took. The battery afterwards invited him to their quarters to dinner on their return to Newbern. I remember a remark Captain Conwell made to Colonel Walkley after one of the successful charges, in which, however, we had only a minor share. The regiments were cheering, and our regiment was called upon for three cheers. Captain Conwell did not join. Colonel Walkley asked why he did not shout with the rest. "Too many hearts made sad to-day," was his short reply.

As was often the case, our regiment lost more men from disease and exposure than in battle or on the line. The worst experience we had in that campaign was in what was afterwards known among us as the "Gum Swamp expedition." The Confederates had begun to erect a fort and lines of breastworks at a station on the Newbern Railroad, about thirty miles in the interior. We were ordered to dislodge them. The forced march in the advance and the short charge which drove the enemy out of their uncompleted works were but play to the dreadful experiences of the retreat. The prisoners warned us not to leave the highway in that marshy region, but the shells fell too thick in the road and the rear-guard were so continually assailed, that our forces were ordered to take a line of march through the swamp. Miles and miles of muck and tall grass, into which we sank to the knees at every step. Wading in black water, torn by thorns and brambles, without food and no place to rest, we marched in sickening exhaustion. That day in the wild swamp was a fearful experience. Men lay down in the water and died, unable to take another step. Many were assisted by branches of trees out of the water, and left to follow if they could. Captain Conwell insisted on going back into the swamp after two of our men who had straggled

into the thicket and were lost. He came back successful, but without his hat, and with his uniform torn into
rags about his legs and thighs. We had organized a
relief expedition to go after him when he appeared
with one of the men, while the other had been left
where comrades could find him by marks on the trees
leading back. Lieutenant Charles Fay of our company
rescued the survivor, I think. How indelible all those
experiences are! But my comrades will need no re-
minder from me.   *

Our term of service was filled afterwards with monot-
onous garrison duty until near the close, we were
ordered into Virginia to reinforce the army then endeavoring to keep Lee out of Pennsylvania. But
before our term of service was out, General Foster
sent for Captain Conwell, and offered to recommend
him for promotion to the colonelcy in command of a
regiment if he would enter at once upon recruiting
service among the men whose term was about to expire.
Captain Conwell accepted the offer, but so many of his
own company decided to re-enlist with him, and such
jealous objections were raised about his youth, that he
decided to accept a captain's commission. He wrote
to the governor that he did not wish to contend for any
other place. But Captain Conwell was taken sick with
a dangerous fever, and by the time the 2d Massachusetts Artillery was in camp at Readville, Mass., his old

comrades were mustered in and new officers placed
over them. He, however, accepted the command of
another company in the same regiment, with the understanding that his former comrades should be transferred
to his company in exchange for others. But the dis-
arrangement led to much hard feeling among the men,
and the transfer was never made. Captain Conwell's
new men, as soon as they met him, were unwilling to
be exchanged, and clung to him with the same affection
as had been seen in the other company. It appears,
from the account two of the officers have written for
me, that the inauspicious beginning was but an augury
of the difficulties, jealousies and mistakes which were
before him in that campaign. He must have been
greatly disappointed, and have gone to the field reckless and humiliated. His men were almost idolatrous
in their devotion to him, and were as sensitive and
jealous as children at the slightest appearance of an-
ticipated acts or dislike for him on the part of any
officer. He devoted himself to his company and
avoided all other society. When his regiment reached
Newbern, N. C., he was stationed for a time at Fort
Macon with his company, and there he buried himself
in the study of law, except when on duty. Afterwards
he was placed in command of a small fort, at a place
called Newport Barracks, in a district commanded by
that noble soldier, the colonel of the 9th Vermont.

There Captain Conwell came near losing his life. One night when making the "grand rounds," visiting the pickets on the outposts of his district, he went into the forest several miles, to a post called Canada Mills. He was accompanied by his orderly, Mr. Daniel E. Spencer, now an extensive manufacturer of boots and shoes in Worcester, Mass. The night was very dark. They had proceeded about two miles when they heard footsteps on the path before them. "Who comes there?" shouted the captain. There was no reply. Then he directed Orderly Spencer to stand quiet, and he passed around through the wood to reconnoitre. Suddenly he found himself directly among a number of men creeping along the ground in a stealthy manner. Again he called, "Who comes there?" He was answered by a volley fired promiscuously toward the spot. The flash of the firearms revealed a company of Confederates, but in the confusion neither could estimate the strength of the other. Sergeant Spencer leaped bravely forward to his captain's aid. The enemies scattered in a panic. It was so dark that they disappeared like flitting shadows. Mr. Conwell says he owes his life to Mr. Spencer's bravery that night. On reaching the picket post Captain Conwell found that shot had pierced his uniform, and one bullet had struck his watch directly over his heart, and shattered the works and case. It was a narrow escape. One little shot from a revolver or shotgun had entered his right shoulder, but so slight appeared the wound that he did not at the time believe any shot had entered the flesh. But long afterward, when a running sore and blood spitting called attention to the spot, a surgeon (Dr. Clarke of New York) traced the little shot, and it was extracted at the Belleview Hospital in time to save his life.

A short time after that dangerous encounter Captain Conwell became greatly disturbed because the paymaster had not visited the post, and his men were in great need of money. He sent several communications to the head-quarters at Newbern, but no attention was paid to them. At last he started off early in the morning, "without leave or license," to visit the paymaster in person. He left his command in charge of an efficient officer, and there seemed no danger of an advance by the enemy, which the cavalry reported to be picketed over twenty miles away. It was a reckless undertaking to ride all the way to army head-quarters through a Carolina forest accompanied by only one man. But he was determined to go then, and get the pay for his men. That night he ran into an enemy's picket, and barely escaped by swimming a deep, dark creek, with shots spattering about him. On reaching Newbern he reported immediately to head-quarters, and received a severe condemnation for having left his command without written orders. General Palmer, in great anger, ordered him to return without a moment's delay, and said the matter should be reported to General B. F. Butler, then in command of that army corps. There was nothing for Captain Conwell to do but to start back. But his dismay and grief must have been great, on reaching the outposts of Newbern, to learn that the telegraph wires had been cut, and that a large body of the enemy was between him and his post. He endeavored to ride around, and also tried to go by boat down the Neuse. But the Confederate army had captured the whole line of posts. He soon learned by an escaped soldier that his men had been driven out of the works, many killed, and the whole ground was held by the Confederates. Captain Conwell is said to have been so heart-broken that he fell into a dreadful brain fever, and for many weeks lay hovering between life and death in wild delirium.

But the attack on the fort at Newport Barracks, in Captain Conwell's absence, illustrated well the love and confidence of his men. The Confederates approached in an overwhelming body and charged without warning, and the small·body of Union troops, though they stood to their cannon until pulled away by the hands of scores of enemies or shot dead at the breast-works, could hope for nothing in a contest where there were at least fifty enemies to each one of our men in the fight. Those

who could get out of the swarm of Confederates re-
treated across the wide river, and set the railroad bridge
on fire behind them. At the time of the retreat the gold-
sheathed sword, which was presented to Captain Conwell at Springfield, hung on the centre pole in his tent.
The army regulations compelled him to wear a sword
of another pattern, so he kept that in his tent. The
attack of the enemy was so unexpected and sudden
that no one thought of saving anything from the tents.
But a boy from Westfield, Mass., named John Ring,
who was Captain Conwell's private assistant, and was
as devoted to him as to his own father, thought of the
sword after they were all across the river. He started
back against many protestations, and rushed along the
blazing bridge, into the very thickest swarm of the
excited Confederates. His bravery saved him then.
They did not notice the unarmed boy. He rushed into
the burning tent and seized the sword. With it hugged
close to his bosom, he ran into the conflagration on the
long bridge. It was a daring deed. Often Mr. Conwell speaks of it with tears. The boy gave his life to
save his loved captain's sword. The smoke, the excitement and the exposure were too great; he succeeded
in getting across the bridge alive before it fell, but
after being carried to Beaufort on a gun carriage, he
died. His last request of his nurse was, "Send the
captain his extra sword." Johnny Ring was a noble

Christian boy. All who knew him loved him. His death was kept from Captain Conwell for some time.

On Captain Conwell's recovery the old feelings against him as a boy were aroused among his competitors, and he was severely condemned for having been "absent from his post without leave." The blame for the defeat must fall somewhere. General Butler was informed that things might have been better if all the officers had been at their posts. He ordered that all such should be brought before a court of Inquiry. Mr. Conwell made no effort to screen himself; he was but a boy; his soldiers were far away. Alone he waited, and cared but little, apparently, what was done.

In the meantime General Foster recommended him for promotion to the command of colored troops. A commission as major in a regiment of native North Carolina white troops was offered him and declined. At last, seeing that all seemed so determined on his destruction, he, reckless as ever, left the whole matter and refused to appear but once at the hearing. But General Foster wrote to General McPherson, then in command of the Seventeenth Corps, and earnestly interceded for an appointment for "a boy who is as brave as an old man." Captain Conwell was directed to report to Washington. But that interference by others prejudiced the local officers naturally, and the hearing went against Captain Conwell. But he saw that an influence like that of General McPherson's would be worth more than legal technicalities, and away he went again "without leave or license." General Butler considered it discourteous, as it was, for generals in other corps to meddle with his men, and was turned by that against the young boy captain. But afterwards, when the finding was reversed by order of the President, on General Butler's own generous recommendation, General Butler made a chivalrous expression of his admiration for Captain Conwell that gave us soldiers a thankful feeling. The State of Massachusetts afterwards gave Captain Conwell, a certificate for faithful and patriotic services in that same campaign. Captain Conwell went to Washington, and the President sent him to General McPherson. It was a number of weeks after he reached Nashville, Tenn., before he could get up to the front, and he first met General McPherson, I think, just before the battle of Kennesaw Mountain. Anyhow, at Kennesaw Mountain he acted as bearer of despatches over the field, and received the most terrible wounds of his service from a bursting shell. He was left for dead all night on the side of the mountain. Mr. John M. Crooks, of Dubuque, Ia., lay near him also wounded, and he writes that he put his head "on Lieutenant Col. Conwell's body in shifting his position, and thought the boy was dead." But when carried into Marietta, at the advance next day, the bones of his arm and shoulder were set, and he was soon able to travel.   •

He was at General McPherson's head-quarters when the advance was made on Atlanta from the Chattahoo-chee River, and went back toward Nashville to recover from his wounds.   He went back to Tennessee with General Thomas, and when his commission was made out as lieutenant colonel, General McPherson was dead, and he was recommended to report to General Logan at Washington.   On the way his weak system broke down at Harper's Ferry, and after several days of hesitation, he heeded the advice of his friends and left the service.   A few months later, and before he had recovered, the war was ended by Lee's surrender.

For nearly ten years after, Col. Conwell was an acute sufferer in consequence of his wounds, but in later years appears to be fully recovered.   How glad all his old comrades are to meet him at the reunions, and to see him so well!

The writer of this sketch has watched Col. Con-well's course with affectionate interest.   I can see that others show the same interest in him, and are equally glad that his life is spared to us and to the Grand Army of the Republic of which he has been such an influential member.

CHAPTER VII.

THE LAWYER.

The boy's "first case"—The best witness—His marriage—Life in Minnesota—Editor—Politician—Young Men's Christian Association—Visits Europe—Return to practice in Mass.—Defending the poor—Free practice—A deceitful client—Gen. N. P. Banks—Pension cases—Narrow escape from death.

RUSSELL was an arbitrator from childhood. In the school-children's quarrels, and in the differences among the young people Russell was continually made the referee. But he once related at a banquet in Boston of the lawyers of that city this incident which led him into the legal profession.

In addition to the farm and produce dealing, Russell's father kept a little country store for the sale of shot and powder to the hunters, groceries to the farmers, and nick-nacks to the children. Of course it was a rude and limited merchantile venture. One day a justice of the peace from Northampton held a hearing in the store. The flour barrel was the judge's bench, and a soap box and a milking stool were the lawyer's seats at

the bar.   Russell sat on the little counter and watched
the proceedings.   The Boston *Post* in its report of Mr.
Conwell's funny description said :

" The green country boy lay flat on his breast on the
counter, with his heels in the air and his chin resting in
both hands.   The case was a complicated suit in re-
plevin, and the hearing was in the form of interroga-
tories, and blanks for depositions to be used in court
afterwards.

Col. Conwell's description kept the whole party in
convulsions of mirth.   The Squire's absurd decisions
and the country lawyer's foolish technicalities, and the
gaping gaze of the rustic denizens of those valleys.
Mark Twain's iron dog would have giggled."

The case had not proceeded far when Russell's interest was awakened to a most excited extent.   It
appeared that an officer was sent after a calf said to be
wrongfully taken, and he had been resisted by the
owner who declared the calf they were after had never
been off his farm.   It was clear before the hearing had
gone far that there was some confusion as to the identity
of the calf in question.   The plaintiff had lost a calf
with a broken horn and a white face.   But the defendant declared that he had never seen that heifer at all,
and the one with a broken horn and white face which
was seen in his barn was one he had raised from birth.
But the defendant was getting the worst of it for the
descriptions tallied so exact.   And he " was also seen

driving a white faced calf up the mountain one night just after the calf had been missed from the pasture." The defendant swore to his deposition, and swore at the attorney, and finally cursed the judge. The case was certainly lost, and the defendant was a thief and a liar, to all appearances. Just then Russell scrambled off the counter, regardless of the disturbance in Court, and in a few minutes appeared at the door with a white faced calf with a broken horn, and in great haste he pushed the dumb witness squarely into the middle of the Court. It was the lost heifer. Russell had found it with his father's cows, and had driven it to the barn and kept it for three weeks, unable until that moment to find an owner. The owner recognized it at once, and gave up the suit and paid the costs. The calf itself was a convincing witness that the other calf was not stolen or taken by mistake.

There was a great deal of fun and talk over the matter, and in the little knot of villagers, Russell was quite a hero. Every old lady said the boy would be a lawyer. It aroused his pride and ambition. From that time the boy was ever swinging back and forth in his purposes between the ministry and the law. So he read about both, and studied the books of both.

In 1865, after he had received his diploma from the Albany University, Col. Conwell was married, at Chicopee Falls, Mass., to Miss Jennie P. Hayden,

daughter of Elizur B. Hayden.   Miss Hayden had been
one of his scholars in a district school in West Granville, Mass., and afterwards one of his most proficient
students of music.   Her brothers, Sydney and William,
were in Col. Conwell's command, and were brave
soldiers, and his true friends.   Her youngest brother, J.
Orlin Hayden, now proprietor of the Somerville *Journal*,
and county treasurer at Cambridge, Mass., was, after
his father's death, employed by Col. Conwell in his
publishing and legal business in Minnesota.

Immediately after his marriage Col. Conwell went
to St. Paul, Minn., and after a few months stay, made his
permanent residence in Minneapolis.   He opened a
law office in a two story stone building on Bridge Square,
over a drug store.   Being poor, he could not wait long
for clients without getting deeply in debt, so with his
usual felicity, he turned his hand to any honest work
which would give him and his young wife a living.   He
acted as agent for his intimate friends, the Thompson
Brothers of St. Paul, in the sale of land warrants.   He
also began to negotiate for the sale of town lots, and
acted as local correspondent for the St. Paul *Press*.   He
was soon in local politics, and canvassed the settlements
and towns for the Republican and Temperance tickets.
He was associated in the work with many of the best
known statesmen of Minnesota.   The friendship of
many of the Congressmen and Senators was of great

use to him in after years.　He was an earnest advocate of the public schools, and was a frequent visitor at the city and district schools.　He was hopeful, active and beaming with fun.

His first law case was as Attorney for himself, and the Justice said, " the young fellow had no fool for a client " even if he did plead his own case.　One of his neighbors who furnished me with the facts, says that Col. Conwell was the popular president of a skating park organization, which kept a large spot on the Mississippi River clear of snow for skating above St. Anthony's Falls, and around Henepin Island.　A contract was made with a rollicking Irishman to scrape the ice when necessary, but the fellow got drunk, and a carnival had to be postponed.　Col. Conwell refused to sign an order to pay the delinquent, and the whole company, including a hundred young men, were sued at law by the Irishman.　They all marched up to court, and the scene was the town talk for fun for a long time. After the Irishman had testified amid shouts of laughter in the unruly court room, Col. Conwell raised the point that there were another hundred citizens who were not joined as defendants who belonged to the company. Then the amused old Justice dismissed the case.

Col. Conwell and his wife had but one room for a home, and that was back of his office on the same floor. There they cooked, ate and slept.　In his law office at that time was begun the business men's daily noon prayer meetings, which resulted in a permanent organ- ization, and which grew into the Minneapolis Young Men's Christian Association.

I have not been able to get much data concerning his law practice in Minneapolis, but I have the belief that it was not very extensive. He was a perfect genius for continuous hard work, but how he could have done all the different things they say he was engaged in will always be a wonder. He soon made money enough to purchase a home, and a large law library, both of which were destroyed by fire.

When Col. Conwell was attacked by a hemorrhage of the lungs on account of his wounds breaking out afresh, he was the owner of many corner lots, the proprietor of a daily and weekly paper called "Conwell's Star of the North," and conducted a job printing office, besides his law business. But he was compelled to drop all business instantly and go away. Governor Marshall, one of his political friends, sent him as Emigration Agent to Europe, but he was too ill to do much, and after reaching Leipsic resigned, and occupied his mind taking lectures several months at that German University. All his business was sold out in Minneapolis at an awful loss, and before he was able to earn his living again he had spent all, and was sadly in debt. He did not re- turn to Minneapolis except to settle some business affairs, and attend the state encampment of the G. A. R. of which he had been Inspector General. When his years of pilgrimage over the world as a traveling correspondent had restored his health entirely.

Col. Conwell began the practice of law again in Somerville, Mass., near Boston. There too he began to purchase and sell real estate. But he was very poor when he began, and lived in the cheapest manner in a tenement. When his first child (a daughter) was born they were actually too poor to own the furniture of one room. But his work as a correspondent and editor enabled him to furnish a home soon after he moved to Somerville. But his law practice prospered there. He was so well known as a public speaker that clients filled his office at once. In a few weeks he was crowded with cases. His ill fortune turned to good fortune, and he was for a time on the road to wealth again. If he had given his chief attention to making money he must have been very rich. But his experience and taste of the bitterness of poverty aroused in him a burning sympathy with the poor. He was often led into large real estate speculations, and one of his clerks told me that he lost fifty-one thousand dollars in one venture during the financial panic of 1874. That disgusted him with real estate speculations. He often endorsed for friends, and one of them failed owing him nearly ten thousand dollars. He could make money, but his unfortunate friends would usually spend it for him.   Then, as I have said, he was a friend to the poor.   Hundreds of cases he managed in the lower courts, and refused the fees, and sometimes paid the expenses himself.

For some years he kept his law office in Boston open every evening and gave counsel and legal work free to any poor person who came. It was a noble charity. Many a poor widow secured her dower, and many a poor orphan obtained their inheritance who had no money or friends otherwise to secure their rights.

It was considered by many what the lawyers call "unprofessional" for him to give his advice free, and many jealous ones accused him of selfish motives; but the students in his law office uniformly say that he never took a case afterwards into court for pay which came to him from the evening charity work. Some evenings he had more than fifty applicants who wished redress for wrongs, or information how to protect them-selves from wrong doers. His advertisement in the Boston daily papers after his office was removed to that city I have kept. It is as follows:

"LEGAL ADVICE FOR THE POOR.

Any deserving poor person wishing legal advice or assistance will be given the same free of any charge, any evening except Sunday, at No. 12 Rialto Building, Devonshire St. None of those cases will be taken into court for pay."

Another remarkable thing about his practice was that neither he nor his law partners would ever take a case into court if their client was in the wrong, nor into the criminal trials if the defendant was guilty. No offers of money could bribe him to do it. It is an honor to our old Commonwealth that such lawyers can still be found practicing at the bar. But the fact that it was known that he would not take a case he knew was wrong, made villains the more anxious to secure him. I do not suppose he escaped deceit always.

One case which leaked out, and was published at the time in the Boston *Sunday Times*, made much fun for Col. Conwell's colleagues. A young fellow who appeared like a saint, convinced lawyer Conwell that he was not a pickpocket as charged. Col. Conwell was certain of the young man's perfect innocence, and went to the District Attorney to urge that the innocent man should not have his name in the papers. When the case came up for trial, Col. Conwell and his client sat close together. After he had addressed the court, it was at once agreed that the case should be dismissed, by the district attorneys consent. So lawyer and client walked out of court triumphantly. When they reached Col. Conwell's office, the defendant paid the fee out of his

lawyer's own pocket-book which he had stolen while
Col. Conwell was stoutly asserting his innocence to
the court. The reckless thief told of it, and returned
the pocket-book afterwards.

During those years of most arduous toil, he started
from his home in Newton Centre at five o'clock in the
morning regularly, and by the time his clerks and
students came to his office, he had the day's work of
each carefully laid out. It was a life of work, work,
work. No rest. Yet his income from his law practice
was very small. It was also at times very perplexing.
Other attorneys thought he was getting rich. The
poor who paid him nothing insisted on believing that
he was paid by some rich charitable institution. Often
the ungrateful clients would abuse him for his ridged
adherence to the right.

One man with whom he sat up whole nights to save
him from the delirium tremens, and whose fine in the
court Col. Conwell paid, was a common example. He
wanted to borrow money. Col. Conwell would not lend
it. The drunkard became angry, and attempted to
stab Col. Conwell to the heart. The colonel knocked
the assassin down with a heavy notarial seal, and then
carried the bleeding villain tenderly to the hospital,
and oared for him there.

In the personal work of temperance reform he
was always active. He never drank intoxicating

liquors of any kind himself, but he had a sympathy with those who did. He often took drunkards to his own beautiful home in Somerville and in Boston, and dosed them all night. He never passed a reeling man on the street without speaking kindly to him. He was on friendly terms with the bar-keepers also; although he told them in plain terms his estimate of their trade. So, many of his law cases were in defence of the poor inebriates, or for their widows, orphans, or deserted families of drunkards. At one time he was the guardian over sixty orphan children. In one case, I am told by a neighbor, he assumed the guardianship of three boys who were destitute ; and through Col. Conwell's intercession with a distant relative, the boys were remembered in a will which gave them fifty thousand dollars in stock in the Baltimore and Ohio Railroad.

During those years in Boston, he often made political speeches, and was the especial favorite of the workingmen. At one time he was nominated by the Republican party for the State Legislature, but was defeated on the temperance issue. At another time he was persistently urged by the Republican and Workingmen's party, in the Fifth Massachusetts congressional district to accept a nomination for congress, but he refused. General Nathaniel P. Banks was a favorite political friend of Col. Conwell, and in one election Col. Conwell was the manager of the entire campaign, and General Banks, running on an independent ticket, was elected by a most astonishing majority.

Senator Charles Sumner and Senator Henry Wilson both urged his name, without his knowledge, for the Consulship at Naples, Italy, having heard his lectures on Italian history at Cambridge. In matters to be heard by the Legislature, he was often the advocate of cities and towns, and was counted an expert in contested election cases. Yet in the midst of all these cares, he found minutes on the cars, or while waiting for trains to study the languages and the latest works of science. Not a minute lost ; not a wasted hour. No one seemed to consider him a great genius, and none of his friends regarded his unostentatious life as anything remarkable. He himself was the last person who would have thought he had any unusual gift. He shunned public praise. He hated flattery, and always avoided those persons who pestered him with compliments after any success.

Catholics, Jewish, Protestant and non-sectarian charities sought his aid in legal matters, and found a ready helper. But in none of them would he ever take an office. In such legal work he was often assisted by General B. F. Butler, for whom he always felt an earnest friendship, because the General was a vigorous, though not always a consistent friend of the laboring classes. Dr. George B. Loring, recently United States Commissioner of Agriculture, was also his friend and pressed him forward in his lectures and practice.

I have written to Mr. Conwell to ask him more of the details of this time in the history of his life, and all the satisfaction I received was a friendly letter in which he says he has forgotten all about it, and " no one cares anything about it anyhow." But it seems to me that this is important. If a person becomes successful in this world, it is helpful to beginners to. know how it is done. The children of our comrades will read this history when we are gone, it may be.

Much of his attention was taken up by applicants for pensions, and his political influence added much to his prestige. Soldiers, orphans, widows and parents applied to him, and his sister says that he could not travel on the cars, or visit his old home without being beset with applicants for a pension. He never charged a soldier, or a soldier's widow a cent for all his work. Sometimes he went to Washington for the sole purpose of securing for some sick comrade the Government's aid. His acquaintance with the Presidents whose biography he had written, and his friendships among the members of congress, made him ever a

successful advocate.   His partners say he never lost
a pension case, nor ever made a cent by it.

He prepared and presented many bills to Congressional Committees at Washington, and appeared as
counsel in several Louisiana and Florida election cases.
His arguments before the Supreme Courts in several
important patent cases were reported to the country by
the Associated Press.   He had at one time considerable
influence with the President and Senators in political
appointments, and some of the best men still in government office in this state (Massachusetts) and in other
New England States, say they owe their appointment to
his active friendship in visiting Washington in their be-
half.   But it does not appear that through all these
years of work and political influence that he ever
asked for an appointment for himself.   I do not think
he ever did.

At one of the dinners in 1878, which was attended by
some of the Alumni of Albany University, Mr. J. B.
Lougee of Syracuse, referred in flattering terms to
Mr. Conwell's success, and said that "the Col. showed
in his legal practice that same forgetfulness of self
which he exhibited in a scene in Connecticut in 1872,"
which the speaker witnessed.   I have tried to get the
full account of it from Mr. Conwell, but he declined
to furnish it.   I have found in the Hartford *Courant,*
October 25, 1872, the following:

"RUNAWAY IN PLAINVILLE—GALLANT CONDUCT OF
COLONEL CONWELL.

While two young ladies by the name of Cullows were driven out by a coachman, Wednesday morning, the horses took fright at an approaching train, and, dashing through the fence, started at a furious speed across a rocky field. The cowardly coachman leaped from the front seat and let go the reins, leaving the ladies to their fate. Colonel R. H. Conwell, the orator and writer of Boston, saw the condition of affairs and bravely rushed to the rescue. He overtook the team, after they had broken the shaft and just as they were making a short turn, which must have crushed the ladies with the carriage, had he not seized the horses by the bridles. He is a powerful man, but so great was their headway that he was carried over rocks and ditches, a distance of more than a hundred yards, and when the exhausted horses were finally stopped, their heads bled profusely where the harness straps cut in, and the Colonel was bruised and his clothing torn, and injured internally so severely that a physician was called, who for a while feared a fatal result. The ladies escaped without a scratch, but the carriage was almost a total wreck. The Colonel is doing well at this writing, but could not fill a lecture engagement which he had at Plainville, Wednesday night, as the physician would not let him be removed."

Not one of our comrades will be surprised at Col. Conwell's action in the above case. Lawyer Lougee's use of the incident as an illustration of his whole life was true to his nature. Such a disposition was clearly apparent in the whole course of his legal business life.

[*Note.*—The following chapters are added entire to the foregoing account.—ED.

CHAPTER VIII.

THE TRAVELER.

*India — Companions — Feeling at home — Descriptions —
Babylon — Gethsemane — Pictures of history — Habits
of travel — Testimony of friends — The English press —
His different journeys — Narrow escapes — Letter from
the battle fields — Lookout mountain.*

M R. LEMUEL T. HARRIS of New York who is mentioned in Mr. Conwell's book on the Chinese, as a traveling companion in an expedition to the Tomb of Confucius, was Mr. Conwell's companion for a long time in other Eastern countries beside China. Mr. Harris died in 1880, but his daughter kindly furnishes the following letter preserved from her father's spicy, private correspondence :

Conwell and I reached Delhi this morning, and have spent the day calling on the " Great Moguls." The remnants and odds and ends of the old Indian royalty. Queer lot. I've had no end of fun. Conwell is the funniest chap I ever fell in with. He sees a thousand things I never think of looking after. When his letters come back in print I find lots in them that seems new to me, although I saw it all the time. But you don't see the fun in his letters to the papers. The way he adapts himself to all circumstances comes from long travel. But it is droll. He makes a salaam to the defunct kings, a neat bow to the Sudras and a friendly wink to the Howadji in a way that puts him cheek-by-jowl with them in a jiff. He beats me all out in his positive sympathy with these miserable heathen. He don't seem to act ever for fun. But it makes much for me. I tell you—if I had the money I would stick to Conwell for five years. He has read so much that he knows about everything. The way the officials, English too, treat him, would make you think he was the son of some lord. He has a dignified condescension in his manner that I can't imitate. But he is a good fellow, and I am glad I met him at Omaha, as I did. I have laughed more at his jokes and stories this past week in the Himalayas than I have laughed before for five years. Even the Parsees treated us as old friends. The contemptible chairman and wild bushman or woodsman, open their dirty huts to him and shut me out. But I don't care to go into many of them. Dirty lot. But he sees and learns all, and all the little naked ninnies cry after him. What comic things he makes them do. He really does like them. They are all jolly with him. I don't think his letters do him justice. I see by the last copy of the *Traveller* that he accuses me of all the funny things. But you can see Conwell more than me. We are going down to Agra, and across to Bombay. I think Conwell will let me go up to Bagdad with him if the *Tribune* writes to him to go. I shall stick to him as long as I can. I had a chill again at Calcutta. But Conwell is a splendid nurse. . . .

We have concluded to go up the Ganges to the "Missionaries Retreat" where George H. Stewart of Philadelphia has been building a hospital, I think. Conwell wishes to write about that, and see the Hurdwar falls. I may not write again for two weeks.

The above letter gives some idea of Mr. Conwell as a traveler, and shows something of his power to win his way among savage people. But his traveling began with a European trip when he was residing in Minnesota, and an extended tour to Palestine, Egypt and the Euphrates when his health failed the following year. It must have been a delightful thing to him to travel. His imaginative powers are brilliant and clear. He seems actually to live, for the time in the scenes of the past. Thousands of listeners will recall the vivid description of the fall of Babylon in his lecture on "Lessons of Travel." The President of Harvard College wrote of it "It is impossible to forget such gorgeous descriptions. The speaker must revel in a series of grand visions." That was a gift which must have been a continual feast to him. He seemed to witness the events of ages gone, as actually moving about him in panoramic view. Mr. Household of Greensburg, Pa. who visited the Paris Exposition of 1868 with Mr. Conwell, says, " Mr. Conwell was a most fascinating traveling companion. He saw beauty and interest in everything."

Mr. Conwell has kindly offered to place at our disposal, any of his correspondence during his journeys, but he seems to have taken no pains to preserve his writings, and we have to go to other sources, in the main, for information. His lecture on "Lessons of Travel" has given us many hints which we have tried to follow up, and in it he says, "The ability to make the present transparent, so as to see through it, into the events of the past seems to be a necessary gift in travel."

Mr. Conwell possessed it in an unusual degree. He visited the ruins of Kenilworth Castle in England, and his excited description of the scenes of poor Amy Robsart's love and death, made the vision clearer to the American traveler than did Walter Scott himself. Every tower stood again complete. The banquet hall was furnished.—The guests were there.—It is night.— Leicester whistles.—Amy starts.—The trap door clicks. —Death! All seemed to be seen by him. How much such scenic power must add to travel. He has often described the battlefield of Waterloo with a detail and graphic power that was far finer and more real to his auditors than a great painting.

"The Picturesque Orator," as he has come to be called, originated in this marvelous gift. He could see the battle: and it must have been real to him. Any listener to his portrayal of the old guard's last charge which sometimes is given in his lecture on "Acres of Diamonds" must be able to see it all as vividly as the real scene could be. Wherever he went it was so. Egyptian tombs gave up their dead, and the catacombs sent out their inmates to live and act their ancient deeds before him. Every battle was fought over, and every forum awoke again with the voices of ancient orators. Each palace hall was peopled again with beauty and chivalry. He could see them, hear them, love and hate them. The present was the far off, and the ancient was the nearest to view. In his letter to the Boston *Times* on his visit to the Garden of Gethsemane, near Jerusalem, he shows what travel was to him.

"Last night we sat in the moonlight, under the old Olives in Gethsemane. The old monk was very kind, and could speak German readily. He was full of traditions and speculations; but when the shadows of the walls began to creep up the side of Olivet, I lost myself in delicious reveries. The monk talked on, the olive trees shook in the breeze, and the cry of some sentry or shepherd often echoed around the walls.

"But all grew indistinct and unreal. All changed about me with transformations like a clear dream. I stood alone in old Gethsemane. No wall of masonry about it, no picket enclosures within. The olives were larger, the hedge deeper, and the Keedron rippled by. Palestine had been hot and disagreeable, but the beds of earth and stone, the poor food, the beggars, the lepers, the guides, the quarreling Arabs, the weeping Jews of the present, with all their disagreeable associations of the present, were gone. I stepped back eighteen hundred years and 'more. It was dark. Lights flashed from the dark outline of the walls. Suddenly the moon looked down through a rift of deep clouds.

"Then it was dark again. The distant mountains beyond the city, and Olivet behind me were strangely outlined against the murky sky. I could hear the voices of pilgrim parties murmuring in their little camps, and the distant chatter of passing travelers going up the steep ascent to the city. . . .

" I saw the shadowy forms of men crossing the little bridge, and saw them indistinctly as they paused at the gateway of the garden. I saw the four come into the garden, and heard their voices. Distinctly one said, as he left the others, under the largest Olive 'Tarry thou here, while I go yonder to pray.' He paused near me. His white robe brushed the vines along the path. Under the next olive he knelt down. The moon came out again and sprinkled his robe with light through the leaves. His head was uncovered. His hands were stretched upward. How pleading his tones in, ' Let this cup pass from me.' What a view of him I had. I cried. Tears came down. I held my breath as the noble man walked back, and woke the

sleepers. Then again he glided by. Again he prayed.
Once more the moon showed him clearly kneeling
there. Oh, what a sight! He was moaning, and had
fallen prostrate on the ground. Suddenly a soft glow,
as of a crimson dawn, grew brighter about the place.
It grew speedily into light which encircled the praying
one. Then softly outlined at first, but quickly defined,
a bright form appeared bending over the weeping
worshiper. An angel! Oh, such divinity of beauty.
Such delicacy of manner. Such grace of motion. Such
compassionate love. I knelt before the vision. I put
my head to the ground. My soul was filled with an
ineffable thrill of heavenly joy. That was worship
indeed. . . . 'Kommen sie mit mir, Mein Herr?'
'You must be dreaming, and very tired,' kindly
commanded the Monk, and the delicious vision was
dissipated. Such scenes long gone, and not the
present landscapes, make the chief joy and profit of
travel."

With such a mind, filled with the accumulated information of incessant study, and with such an imagination,
his experience as a traveler must have been thrilling.

From the Dead sea to the sea of Gallilee, and up the
Jordan's cliffs, he must have found a continual feast.
From Capernaum to Nazareth and to Damascus, the
old associations must have enriched him. Even the
desert route to Palmyra, and the other trip to Sinai and

Mecca had a fascination to him which a different disposition could never feel.

On the upper Nile, on the Yangtse in China, he was ever in close communication with the characters of the past. In Sweden and Russia, as in Greece and Italy there were scenes as Bayard Taylor said of him. " Which he understood where the unread pilgrim saw nothing but dust." The Turk and Austrian, the Bulgarian and Caucassian were human friends to him. Their Mythology and history he seemed to know by instinct. Henry M. Stanley of the New York *Herald*, and Edward King of the Boston *Journal* used an almost identical expression in writing of him from Paris in 1871. " Send that double-sighted yankee, and he will see at a glance all there is and all there ever was."

At a grand banquet given to the Western Editors in New Orleans, at which Mr. Conwell was a specially invited guest, the editor of the Mattoon [Ill.] *Journal* said, " That man finds more of real romance in our matter-of-fact world than any poet in the world."

But his descriptions did him injustice, often. He wrote his letters on carts joggling over rough roads, or in some rude cabin. A hut or a palace was all the same to him. He wrote hastily and rudely often. Sometimes he was so independent as to be offensive, and was often too well acquainted with men's ancestry and history, and he was often careless and hasty. There was no other writer like him, and he had a style no one would be inclined, perhaps, to copy, and he saw that the attractiveness of his writings did not lie in their rhetorical merits. He was often urged by friends to publish in a book his celebrated " Russell's letters from the Battle Fields," written for the Boston *Traveller*. But he would never consent. He never seemed to take any pride in them. To one who looks over his writings, from whatever quarter of the world they come, there is the same appearance of entire carelessness of literary effect, as though each letter was for a private note to be read but once and thrown away. In 1878 he showed a party over Europe, and among them was Miss Sophia B. Packard, Principal of the Spellman Female Seminary at Atlanta, Georgia. Miss Packard said of him in Boston in 1880: "His way of leading the tourists up to an interesting locality, and his graphic introduction, made the journey a panorama of exciting views."

At the time of Mr. Conwell's second visit to England as a correspondent, the London *Times* said of him. "Col. Russell H. Conwell, who has been making a journey entirely around the world, sailed for home last week. Col. Conwell is one of the most noteworthy men of New England. He has already been in all parts of the world. He is a writer of singular brilliancy and power, and as a popular lecturer his success has been astonishing. He has made a place beside such orators as Beecher, Phillips and Chapin." This notice, with many others from the English Press kindly furnished us from the Lecture Bureau, show the esteem in which as a traveler he was held.

Mr. Conwell has crossed the Atlantic seven times, and made one entire circuit of the globe. His first trip included a visit to Ireland, Scotland, England, France, Switzerland, Italy, Greece, Jerusalem, Turkey, Austria and Germany.

His second journey took him to France, Italy, Northern Africa, Egypt, Palestine, Babylon, Nineveh, Turkey, Russia, Denmark, Sweden and Scotland.   His third tour included a lecture trip in the western Territories and California, at which time the Mormon Tabernacle was crowded successive nights by an audience admitted only by purchased tickets to hear the distinguished orator. He then went on to the Sandwich Islands, through Japan into the interior of China, and to Pekin, visited Sumatra, Siam, Burmah, Madras, journeyed to the Himalaya Mountains, through India, pierced Arabia to Mecca, went to the Upper Nile and came home by the way of Greece, Italy and France. In the third trip to America from France, the steamer Iona was wrecked at sea in a fearful storm, and for twenty-one days floated helplessly in mid-ocean. There was much suffering and the dreadful experience has been often referred to by Mr. Conwell in his addresses and books.

Once, either on his trip to Babylon or in his journey around the world he was quarantined on a steamer in the Red Sea with the cholera on board, several deaths occuring daily. He is said to have had several narrow escapes among savage tribes in the desert, and to have been shot at by gamblers in New Orleans whose pre-cincts he had invaded for news, but we never heard that Mr. Conwell has mentioned them in writing so that the particulars can be found in print.

His next visit to Europe was on a lecture tour, and his last one was at the time of the Paris Exposition [1878] and has been mentioned. It may aid the reader in comprehending our discussion of Mr. Conwell's traits as a traveler if we insert here entire one of his letters from the " Battle Fields " which we find in the Boston *Traveller* of July 13th, 1869. The whole series ought to be collected for publication in book form :

THE BATTLE-FIELDS OF THE REBELLION.
LETTER FROM "RUSSELL."

The mountains and valleys around Chattanooga—The spirit of the hills —The present appearance of Lookout mountain—A poor white family —Chivalry rampant—Seventeenth letter—Special correspondence of the Traveller.

THE MOUNTAINS.

Oh the old mountains ! How we love to gaze upon them and dream ! How our soul fills with unspeakable pleasure as we contemplate the rocky cliffs, and the roaring gorges of the mountains! It is the inspired pleasure which one feels only when he looks upon the mighty works of God. The spirit of the hills and the demons of the mountains! Are they a myth? Nay. Go! ye disbelievers who laugh at ghost stories and fairy tales;—sit beside that sweet waterfall on the cliffy side of

LOOKOUT MOUNTAIN,

and tell us if ye doubt their existence then. Go! sit on the jutting rock that is bathed with the spray, and gaze up at the little stream as it leaps over the rock forty feet above! and then at the snowy spray-cloud that rolls and floats away, away down among the bushes and trees forty feet below. The stout old trees creak and sway in the winds above, the pines down the mountain side moan, and the waterfall laughs. Away through the trees are those other mountains, shadowy and blue, just veiling the sky of the far-off horizon. He that can sit here alone, surrounded by these jagged rocks and monumental mountains, and see no German fairies, English ghosts, Arabian peris, or Norwegian demons hath surely no taste for natural beauty, nor a fit appreciation of the awe-inspiring works of the Almighty. Deny it, ye who may, the mountains do have souls, and their children, the fairies, do have influence upon the destinies of men. Else why is it that the men of the mountains are always hardier, happier and greater lovers of freedom than they of the plains and valleys? Why are the people of the hills more generous, loftier minded and braver than their brethren of the prairie ? If the fairies do not assist their human proteges, how came Switzerland free ? Far, far along the highway of history, who were the conquerers? Who were the patrons of civilization ? Who were the martyrs ? Men of the mountains. Who march into the city with less education, less capital than their competitors, and soon lead the march toward the land of plenty and wealth? Who came down from the North and the West and on the cragged side of this same mountain gained a Switzerlandish victory? The men of the fairy-filled mountains. Men of the city die off, and men of the hills, floating down on the roaming cataracts, fill their places. On the ocean, in the warehouses, on the rostrum, in the halls of legislation, in the army or on the throne, the men of the mountains are found, rugged as their native hills, as high minded as their mountains, and as generous as their valleys are deep. Don't say, then, that there is no spirit of the hills, or that there are no fairies. Wherever the mountains are grand and the chasms deep, wherever the waterfalls tinkle or the torrent bellows, there dwell the little beings that influence man's character. Do you say it is only the mountains? How can cold dirt make men better or

wiser? But be it fairy or hob-goblin, dirt or rock, men
do become braver and nobler for dwelling in the
mountains. Hence

NEW ENGLAND'S POSITION

in the nation. Hence the reason why her ideas and
actions are noted and imitated everywhere within the
borders of this nation. Oh, glorious mountains ! safe-
guard of American freedom ! go on with your divinely
appointed mission. For while you stand, and while
the granite melts not or the waterfalls cease not,
freedom will be the watchword, at least in all New
England. And here to, in East Tennessee, how the
men of the mountains fought for liberty during the war
of the rebellion. Here they dared everything. Here
they were robbed, slandered and murdered. But yet
firm as these high peaks, their survivors fought on.
To be a union man then meant death. What was that
to them? The mountains taught them the value of
freedom and did not leave them nerveless in the
presence of the Eastern Tennessee hot-beds. Here,
too, came the men of the hills to conquer slavery and
rebellion. They were at the bottom of a mountain
nearly a mile in height, looking up to the cliffs. Brave
natives of the plains were on the top and glaring down.
Yet the spirit of the mountains came up and conquered.
Do the boys remember that Lookout Mountain battle?

Gen. Hooker himself did not believe it could be done. "Tell them to come back," shouted the General in command. But no notice of orders directing a retreat was taken, and onward and upward they went, climbing precipices, rocks and trees, swinging up to the edge of ledges,—pulling one another up among the clouds,—caring nothing for the hideous shell that came crashing down among the trees, until the citadel was taken, and one more victory for freedom was recorded in the world's history. Grand old mountain! Grand old soldiers of a grand old people! How proud of our nation, our country and our people, were we, the day we visited Lookout Mountain. The changes were many which intervened between that immortal day and the day when we were there. The rifle-pits which Hooker's Division carried and from which his forces charged up the mountain had nearly all washed away; enough was left, however, to mark the direction of the line, and recall to mind the terrible events of

"That great avenging day."

But, farther up

THE MOUNTAIN'S SIDE,

the trees and moss have grown anew, the bushes which the soldiers uprooted as they pulled themselves up have decayed and given place to others, and nothing remains to remind us of war. "Nothing!" did we say? Not

so. Under a little pine tree, near the precipitous-
ledge, which the " boys " will remember, we found

A HUMAN SKELETON.

We were pulling ourselves along up the edge of the
rock, and finding our footing insecure, we seized upon
a proffered branch of a neighborly pine. Up it came
by the roots, taking with it the thin scale of soil which
covered the rock, and exposing to the sun the grinning
skull of a Union soldier. Near it was an old Springfield musket, covered with rust and broken in twain
near the lock. The bayonet, so blackened and tar-
nished that we first took it for a stick, was thrust
into the ground near the skull, and the finger bones lay
about it as if the soldier had clasped it when he died.
A bundle, which had evidently been a knapsack, lay a
few feet off, and had the appearance of being in use as
a bird's nest. For the little pieces of the blue overcoat
and threads of the gray blanket were neatly arranged
in the shape of a nest, which, however, had been torn
by a fox or other marauding animal. In all proba-
bility the little bird made her nest in the decaying
knapsack, and the little four-footed enemy of birdly
innocence came, and in the presence of the soldiers'
bones, broke the eggs and killed the songster. It was
a matter of surprise to us that the wild beasts which
came so near to search for eggs, should not disturb the

bones of the lost soldiers. A few pieces of the spinal column lay scattered around, but otherwise the skeleton was entire. Near the spot we found a U. S. Infantry button, and the soles of a pair of shoes, but nothing to identify the man who gave his life for the nation, in that fearful charge. Whose son or brother he was, whose husband or father, eternity alone can tell! Yet we could not avoid the thought as we stood gazing upon the sad scene, that perchance somebody who read the *Traveller*, or some one we personally knew, might be the dearest one to this soldier of Hooker's corps from whom his friends had never heard.

"Never been heard from," is his record on the page of history! "Dead" in the records of mortals. "In heaven" we hope in the records of eternity. With no implements to bury them, and no soil deep enough if we had, we could not do otherwise than clamber on, leaving the bones to be ground into dust by the merciless hand of time.

PULPIT ROCK

from which Jeff Davis harangued the Confederates, and near which the rebels had some of their heaviest guns, appears as familiar as an old friend, and seems to smile in derision at the changeable growth and decay that has been going on around. The shell-split trees have recovered from their wounds, the earthworks have washed away, the hospital buildings and negro huts are gone, yet the old rock stands on the summit like a sentinel, and will stand there in the hundred years to come, to tell the story of the slave-holding rebellion, and the charge of the national troops. To us, whose pride had been touched in the days of war, it seemed to say. "When I remind visitors of the battle, I also insinuate that below me, the troops of the stigmatized 'paper collar division' rebutted the slurs that the Western troops saw fit to cast upon them for belonging to the spade-and-shovel army of the Potomac." But with the history of rebellion or battles we have little to do, hence we pass on down the eastern slope of the great mountain to ascertain

HOW CHATTANOOGA APPEARS

to-day. The old forts which crowned every hill around the little town, look like the Indian mounds of Illinois; no regularity, no apparent design. Little artificial hills and valleys only. Few soldiers, were it not for the ever-lasting hills around, which God made, would recognize the forts they garrisoned; so torn and shattered, decayed and washed are they now. A few years and even these red mounds will have disappeared and the "great railroad centre" of Chattanooga will not dream of battle or siege. The town itself has not recovered from the war, *i. e.*, unless it always had a forsaken, slovenly appearance. Removing the tents, the barracks, and the stables, and filling the quarter-master's stores and the commissary warehouses with peanuts and candy, soda water and persimmon beer is a sinking in poetry that strikes the returner first as being a little ridiculous.

THE OLD HEAD-QUARTERS,

where Thomas, Grant, Sherman and McPherson had their quarters, still stands near the town house, so unchanged that we felt as if one of them ought to be sitting on the porch.

A new bridge has been built across the river, and the old swing ferry is going to decay.   Cameron's hill, with its washed earthworks, is said to be destined for the grounds and mansion of a Massachusetts man who went to Chattanooga to engage in building the new railroad line South to Charleston, S. C.   Some ruins and dilapidated walls of houses destroyed during the war still remain, although many have been cleared away preparatory to reconstruction.   The old railroad depot still bears the marks of the soldiers' pen-knives, and the name of many a sentinel who wished thus to immortalize it, stands out in bold relief from the soft boards in which it is carved.   The short train of half loaded cars that now come and go, form a striking contrast with the long, over-loaded trains that came and went when Sherman was marching on Atlanta.   The fields around which were covered so thick with tents when Bragg threatened the town, and on which has been so many brigade drills and dress parades, are now verdant with growing grain.

It was exceedingly gratifying amid the many changes that have taken place, to see at least one familiar object. The national flag was there. About half way between Orchard Knob and the town and near the Chattanooga and Knoxville railroad, stands the

NATIONAL CEMETERY,

and above it, in all its pride and glory, waves the ensign of the United States. When we visited the cemetery

A TOUCHING INCIDENT

occurred, which we cannot refrain from putting on record. It was nearly dark. The flag was hauled down, the keeper had shut the gate, and the dew was beginning to fall. We clambered over the fence, and strayed among the graves, endeavoring to find how many of the 2nd and 33rd Massachusetts lay there, supposing ourselves to be the only persons in the grounds. Suddenly from a little clump of graves beyond the flag-staff, a voice as clear and sweet as an angel's rose singing the familiar words,

> " When we hear the music ringing
> In the bright Celestial dome,
> When sweet angel voices singing,
> Gladly bid us welcome home,

To the land of ancient story,
  Where the spirit knows no care,
In that land of light and glory,
  Shall we know each other there ? "

Had a voice from the tomb pronounced the approach
of the last great day we could not have been more
startled—so quiet and still had the cemetery been.
For a moment we stared in the direction from which
the voice proceeded, uncertain whether all the ghost
stories of our youth were not coming true, and hoping
if it was the voice of a spirit that it would wait for us
" to retreat in good order" before it resorted to any
fiercer demonstration to deprive us of our wits. After
a second thought, however, we concluded that it was
the voice of a woman, and as some women are but
our ideals of angels, it did not take much from the
interest of the occasion. Going up to the flag-staff
as silently as we could we sat down upon a mound,
when the second verse began we endeavored to chime
in the bass. In that we were unkind. We ought
to have known that if a woman's voice could startle
us, how much more alarming it would be to a woman
to hear a voice at once suggestive of the men whose
graves surrounded her, singing such a song with
her. But we did not stop to think. Impulse, nothing
else, was our motive. So we sang; with just such
a consequence as any man of common sense might

have foreseen.   SHe had reached the chorus, in which
the bass repeats the words "shall He know," while
the soprano prolongs the sound of the word "know,"
before she seemed to discover that she was not singing alone, and with a shriek as piercing as the song
was sweet, a lady in black started from the grave of
a soldier, exclaiming in hysterics, "What is that?
Oh! Oh! Oh! Don't hurt me! Oh! Oh! Oh!
My God.   Oh dear.   Oh! dear.   Oh! dear.   What
shall I do?"

I "did not intend to frighten you.   I am exceedingly
sorry for it," said I, stepping out from the staff.

"Oh, sir, was it you? Did you sing?" exclaimed she,
wiping her eyes with a handkerchief, and uttering an
hysterical laugh, half cry and half laugh, and looking
wildly toward the gate.

"I do not wonder that my singing frightened you,"
said I, "but it is a question which of us was the most
startled."

So saying, we offered to escort her home, as it was
growing dark.   But this she declined, saying, she
wished to stay a while longer near this spot, as she
"must go to-morrow," and we left her kneeling by the
grave of an Ohio soldier, murmuring again the song
"Shall we know each other there?"   Ten thousand
conjectures have we cooked up in regard to this lady
and why she was there.   But as we did not see her again

and none of our explanations may be the true one, we must leave this tale so far uncompleted.

The next day we strolled along

MISSIONARY RIDGE,

to find such traces as might remain of that great November battle when the troops by unexampled bravery outgeneraled their own officers. But the growth of the woods and the action of the heavy rains have obliterated nearly every mark of the battle, and without a guide a stranger to the field must have great difficulty in finding the "line of battle." Occasionally a shattered tree here and there an old shell in the thicket, and little open spots where works once stood, are all that is left on the spot to tell the tale of war. All the soldiers who were buried here, both federal and confederate, have been taken up and removed to Chattanooga. Near the place where Sherman's division made the "most brilliant charge of the war" we found the

PICKET POSTS,

in some instances just as the soldiers had left them five years ago. Some were of standing logs, one end on the ground and the other leaning against a tree, several of which were placed near enough together to protect the picket behind them, while he rested his gun across the top. In other places short pieces of

stone-wall, or a leaf-filled hole in the ground, showed
where some picket took measures to protect himself.
For hours we traveled, clambering up rocks, over trees,
and through groves, until starting down the mountain
towards Chickamauga creek, we stepped in at

A MUD-CHINKED LOG HOVEL,

to rest and get out of the blistering sun.   The hut was
occupied by a thin, tall woman, about forty years of
age, a man of about the same age, and a little boy of
ten years.   All three were the dirtiest, raggedest
filthiest persons we ever saw north of Georgia. The
woman was sucking a snuff-daubed rag in her mouth,
and snuffing the same nasty material up her nose.
The man's chin and grizzly whiskers were dripping with
tobacco juice, his feet were bare, and on his head was
a remnant of a faded felt hat, while with the old pipe
in his mouth, his general appearance gave us a good
personification of indolence and poverty.   The little
boy seemed to have inherited all the worst character-
istics of them both, which, together with an acquired
taste for swearing and kicking his mother, made him
"master of the position."   When we rapped at the
door the little boy came to the door before his lazy
ancestors could muster sufficient courage to rise, and
kicking our shins demanded if we didn't know better
than to be " around a gemman's house making sich a

cussed row." The old man came, however, and by
means of sundry kicks and cuffs succeeded in quieting
the human animal, and at once invited us in.

"Do you live here?" inquired we for want of anything else to say.

"Wall, ther old ooman and I manage to stop here,"
said the man; "ony Bill here; he's kind o' unsettled.
Bill is kind o' rude sometimes; but sez I ter ther old
ooman t'other day, we mustn't lick Bill as we would a
nigger; and sez she ter me, I don't think I would
nuther. So we don't."

The conversation then turned upon the weather and
several topics, and finally we asked him what he managed to do for a living.

"Der," said he, "I first works round, gits a few dollars huntin' or diggin' wild arbs, and then I cums hum to
ole ooman, and sez I to her, let's 'joy it, and so we 'joy
it. If Bill wan't unsettled, wede be putty good situated. But ther cussed niggers are leavin' or dyin' off,
and some on us are gettin' fraid we'll get starved out
some day."

"I should think you would get a better living if the
negroes were gone," said I.

"O, no. The niggers have always dun the dirty
work, an' all the liftin' an' sich, which as how the white
folks of my persuasion ain't able to do, an' wouldn't ef
ther could. Ther niggers were made to wait on us

white folks, an' I'd like ter know what in the devil ther would do if they didn't look arter white folks. They hain't got nothin'. Ef ther Yankees are goin' ter free them and carry them all off to Lobeli or Liberia, or sumwhar, I be dummed ef I'll do another scratch o' work. Besides ther ole ooman is the same pinnion, an' I'd jest like to ter know what in creation ther government'll do then."

"The negroes are free now," said we, "and over twelve hundred thousand have died off since the war."

He started to his feet in astonishment at the news, exclaiming, "Ther devil! is that so, stranger?"

"Wall," continued he, filling his pipe, and putting in a fresh quid, "I dun know as I care fer ther folks down at the salt water as long as ther folks 'round here don't git white men like me ter dewin nigger's work."

"Do you own this land around here?" inquired we, glancing out of the door.

"Lor', lor' no," said he, apparently astonished at the question, "this land an' cabin allers belonged to Col. Billins, only I've lived in this place ser long he sez ter me tother day, sez he, 'Mr. Farler, yer needn't never move.' So now I 'joy life."

"I should think since the war it would be hard to get a comfortable living," said we.

"No trouble 'tall, none 'tall. The ole ooman an' I an' Bill we eat taters mostly, unless corn be handy;

an' we does it jest ter bring up Bill ter be independent. A man ken live on mighty little ef he jest sets 'bout it. I think more of my terbacker than onything otherwise, an' so does ther ole ooman. So we jest 'joys life."

"Were you in the army?" returned we.

"Lor', no. I 'joyed life ter hum. 'Sides, when I did talk of goin', Col. Billins said as may be I'd hev ter fight 'long er niggers, an' I never could belower myself ter that nohow."

"You would have joined the Northern army then, had it not been for the negroes would you?" asked we.

"Jine ther Yankees!" exclaimed he, excitedly, "Me, a Southerner, born in Marion County, Georgia, an' brought up with 'ligious principles! Put me on a level with niggers and Yankees, an' willinly cum ter be a slave! That's a 'sinuation, sir, agin my character. I'd like ter know how you dare cum inter a gemman's house an' 'sinuate agin his honor as a gemman. I allers defend my honor, sir, with my life, der yer know that?"

"I did not intend to offend you, sir, although I am not afraid of a dozen such white-livered ragamuffins as you are," said we. [A little light brag when taken in the light of subsequent events.]

This was too much for the whole family, and with one accord they arose to attack us. The old man made for the gun which hung on the hooks over the back door, the old woman yelling "Oh, you old coward," seized the iron shovel from the fire-place and the boy rushed up and began to kick at us.   In such a predicament we were not a little puzzled to know what to do. There was only one room in the hut, and the only way out of that was to pass the man with the gun.

"Give me my powder and shot, ole ooman," shouted the man.

"Ole dad is gewin ter salt yer, yer ole white nigger," shouted the son.

But thinking discretion to be, in this instance, the better part of valor, we marched by the old man, telling him he need not load that gun for us; and left the excited chevalier's family all gazing out of the door after us, and shouting, "You're a coward!   Yer insult women and children!   Yer daresn't fight at twelve paces!" etc., etc.   We regarded the ignorant, tobacco-worshiping "poor whites" as little better than wild beasts, and felt easier when their hut was out of sight, as we should have felt had it been a tiger's den we had entered unarmed instead of a human dwelling.   Whatever ridicule we may incur for permitting the representative of the *Traveller* to be so easily defeated we do not know; but we have the satisfaction of knowing that the retreat was conducted in a more masterly manner than many retrograde movements of the war, for which the commanding generals of the army claimed high honors.   RUSSELL."

During his journeys Mr. Conwell often visited General Garabaldi, in Italy, and at his island home. They kept up a correspondence on matters of Italian history until the general's death. General Garabaldi called Mr. Conwell's attention to the heroic deeds of that admirer of America, the great and patriotic Venetian statesman, Daniel Manin. Mr. Conwell spent a long time gathering materials for a biography of Daniel Manin, and just before it was ready for the press the manuscript was destroyed by fire in the destruction of his home at Newton Centre, Mass., in 1880. Mr. Conwell's graphic lectures on Italian history will never be forgotten by his hearers. Whether Mr. Conwell has undertaken to rewrite the life of Daniel Manin, we can not say. Every patriotic American should know the history of that foreigner whose love for this country which he had never visited was so fervent.

CHAPTER IX.

THE MINISTER.

Turning from the world — Beginning to preach — Sunday schools — Missions — Second marriage — The Lexington church building by faith — Generous helpers — The church bell — His ordination — The call to Philadelphia — Church life — Great growth — The new church building — Published accounts.

A S will be seen by the statements following, we are very largely indebted to friends in Boston and in Philadelphia for the information contained in this chapter. It is a romantic turn in an exciting life. When Charles the Fifth abdicated his throne and went into a monastery, the world wondered. It was a like spirit which sent the lawyer and politician into the Christian ministry. All the cherished ambitions of life were thrown aside, and all the hopes of his friends who saw high preferment just before him were disappointed. Sought as an author, praised as an orator, courted as a scholar and successful as a lawyer, he laid down all and completely abandoned all the cherished plans of life. He was thirty-six years old, and

his success was certain in the life he had followed.   In
the ministry all was uncertain.   An entire revolution.
To give up all the expectation of riches and honors,
and to face the criticisms and fears of his best friends,
and turn away to take up an humble mission wherein
there could be neither hope of wealth nor a prospect of
fame, was of the strange things in human life.   He
buried every hope of earthly advancement, and sunk
himself into expected oblivion.   He seemed to deter-
mine to hide himself in Christian work for the poor.
His neighboring preachers say that he shuns office and
prominence, and in the city where his name has become
a household word there are many preachers who have
scarcely seen him.   No hint of honors and no proffers
of gain turn him again to ambitious paths.   A friend
who visited Philadelphia in 1888 wrote, "This seems
almost incredible to me, that the humble, plain man
who is awkward often and simple always is so different from the Col. Conwell we used to know.   He is the
lawyer no more.   You should see him traversing the
alleys in night and rain and cold, and it would be a
surprise indeed, because he seems wholly devoted to
that work.   The dying call for him by night and by
day, and lots of the poor dog his steps for aid.   He
goes at every call, and has forgotten all his old, active, public life."

His change of profession was almost as complete a

renunciation of the world as if he had entered a monastery. Yet the Master Mind who seeth all things has
avenues to nobility closed to all but those who trust
humbly in Him.

Mr. Conwell says that his mind was turned toward the
ministry by the death of his wife in Somerville, Mass.,
in 1871. She left two little children, one daughter (now
married) and a son. They had struggled with an un-
usually varied life, and were just entering a prosperous
period when the wife of his youth died suddenly of
some quick disease. "Vanity! All is Vanity!" was
his cry. He entered then most enthusiastically into
Sabbath school work, and gave addresses at Sabbath
schools all over New England. The children hailed
his coming with delighted faces. He began also to
preach evenings at mission stations, and one of the missions at which he was the first preacher is now the
prosperous West Somerville Baptist Church. He had
studied theology for years, as a pastime or recreation,
so he stepped into the labor full fledged. He went to
any place to preach if there was good before it, and he
often spoke to sailors on the wharves, and to the Sunday loafers he gave sermons from a barrel top. It did
not make much difference where, as his heart turned
toward the sorrowing and the lost. But the event
which set the current into its final channel was his
marriage in 1873 to a lady of a most respected family,

TEMPLE COLLEGE.

Miss Sarah F. Sanborn of Newton Centre, Mass. We have been told that he met the lady at a German mission school in a suburb of Boston, where she was a teacher. It was in the same work they met. Her family were wealthy and influential, and they were also fully christian. Among the intimate friends of her family was the Rev. Alvah Hovey, D. D., President of the Newton Baptist Theological Seminary. It was he who gave Mr. Conwell the quick-witted advice when asked how to decide if "called to the ministry." The reverend doctor said, "If people are called to hear you, then you can safely claim you are called to preach."

Mr. Conwell and Miss Sanborn were married at her brother's fine residence on Seminary Hill, Newton Centre, and immediately took up their residence in Mr. Conwell's new home on College Hill, Somerville, Mass. For a time he continued his law practice and engaged in building enterprises and real estate speculations. But it was all unsatisfactory, and he says that work became merest drudgery. It had no attraction to him, and it seemed to bring only trouble and loss. Providence set its tide against him, and he pulled against the stream. He tried to satisfy his conscience by taking a bible class in the Baptist church at Tremont Temple, Boston. But that only intensified his unrest. His class beginning with four scholars, in a few months numbered six hundred regular registered

attendants. His influence grew too strong. Uncon-
sciously to him, he found petty jealousies arising concerning the influence of the active body of christians
over which he presided because he was not an ordained
minister. As that devoted company showed their love
for him so strongly, he is said to have felt then that he
could do so much more good if he were an ordained
preacher.

Just at that time Mr. Conwell was consulted as a
lawyer concerning the sale of an old building and a
church lot in Lexington, Mass., formerly the property
of an extinct Baptist Society in Lexington. His clients
wished to know how the property could be sold or so
disposed of as to be used in helping christian work
there or elsewhere.

It is said that Lawyer Conwell visited the town first
to call a meeting of former members of the Baptist
Society to get a legal vote to sell out the old building.
Anyhow when the three or four living representatives
of the former society came together they would not
vote either way. One good old deacon wept to think
"Zion had gone into captivity." Mr. Conwell wrote to
a relative in 1880 about it, and said, "It flashed into
my mind, when there as a lawyer, that there was a
mission for me there. The town of Lexington is one
of the finest for location, and for the sterling integrity
of its people, to be found anywhere, and it did seem

sad that the church should fail there. An inspiration came over me to 'Go preach His Gospel' there, and I accepted the first invitation they gave me."

Whether it was a day or an evening service, we do not know, but the residents of Lexington give an amusing account of that first preaching service. There were sixteen or seventeen people in the old decayed structure. The windows were broken, and the plaster hanging in great rifts. The old stove was rusted out at the back, and the stove pipe rusted out in many places. The old pulpit was what Mr. Conwell called a "crow's perch," and the pews were rotted and askew. It was a cold, gloomy, damp, dingy old box, they say. Mr. Conwell preached. It was a new thing to hear a lawyer preaching! He went the second Sunday, and had about forty auditors. But the third Sabbath it had become noised about who was preaching, and the little old chapel was dangerously full. One side of the front steps did tumble down before service. They tried to build a fire, but smoked out all the invalids who came to the meeting. It was rude and uncomfortable. Mr. Conwell has often said that it was that night, when in his own heart he decided that a new church should be built.

It was all a work of faith. For not one step could he see ahead, and not a dollar had the society. And no members who could give anything. Yet he believed that a church could be built. The two or three persons to whom he mentioned his faith that Sunday night all said it would be impossible to build a church there. The revolutionary spirit of their fathers of 1776 was sleeping then. Mr. Conwell and an aged christian man spent that night almost entirely in prayer. In the morning early [Monday] Mr. Conwell bought a pick used on the railroad, and a woodsman's ax, and began the work without a single subscription, and alone. He laid his coat on an old fence, and began work with the pick. The early risers on that Monday morning were astonished to see the lawyer-preacher swinging the pick and tearing away the old rickety wooden steps. Plank, boards and timbers came tumbling down in heaps of ruin. The preacher's blows increased in strength and number as the work went on, and the echo of the ax called the attention of all the passers over that celebrated Lexington road. Some say that it was not fifteen minutes after he began the work, and others say that it was two hours after, and when he was covered with dust and sweat, that the first man accosted him. At all events it was not long after he had begun before a respected citizen of the old town, but one who seldom went to church, came along and, according to a published account, said: "What in the name of goodness are you doing here?"

"There is going to be a new church here," answered the preacher.

"I guess you won't build it with that ax," said the neighbor, laughing at the idea.

"I confess I don't know just how it is going to be done," said Mr. Conwell, "but in some way it will be done."

The spectator shouted at the ludicrous idea, and walked away. He had not gone far before he turned about, and, walking up to Mr. Conwell, seized the axe, and said: "See here, preacher, this is not the kind of work for a parson or a lawyer. If you are determined to tear this old building down, hire some one else to do it. It does not look right for you to be lifting and pulling here in this manner."

"We have no money to hire any one, and the structure must give way if I have to do it all alone," said Mr. Conwell.

"I tell you what I will do," said the visitor, "if you will let this alone, I will give you one hundred dollars to hire some one."

"We would like the money," said the working minister, "and I will take it to hire some one, but I shall keep right on with the work myself."

"All right," said the visitor. "Go on if you have set your heart on it. You may come up to the house for the one hundred dollars any time to-day."

The donor passed up the road. But he was hardly out of sight before a good natured man who disliked churches in general, came along and enjoyed the fun of seeing the minister puff at the heavy timbers.

"Going to pull the whole thing down are you?" said he to Mr. Conwell.

"Yes, sir, and begin all new," answered the minister.

"Who is going to pay the bills?" asked the new visitor.

"I don't know now. But the Lord has money some-where to buy all we need."

The man laughed heartily and said: "I'll bet five dollars to one, you won't get the money in this town."

"You would lose," said Mr. Conwell, " for Mr. —— just came along and gave me one hundred dollars."

"Did you get the cash?" asked the astonished spectator.

"No, but he told me to call for it to-day."

"Well is that so. I don't believe he meant it. Now I'll tell you what I'll do. If you really get one hun-dred dollars out of that man, I will give you another hundred, and pay it to-night."

Then the preacher worked on alone all day. Passers by called, one after another, to ask what was going on. To each one Mr. Conwell told his hope and mentioned the gifts. Nearly every one added something without being asked, and at six o'clock when Mr. Conwell hung up the pick and ax at the end of his day's work he was promised more than half the money necessary to tear down and build a commodious church. But Mr Conwell did not leave the work.   With shovel, or hammer, or saw, or paint brush he worked day by day all that summer along-side the workmen.   He was architect, mason, carpenter, painter and upholsterer, and he directed every detail, from the cellar to the gilded vane, and worked early and late.   The money came without asking as fast as needed.   The young people who began to flock about the faith-worker undertook to purchase a large bell, quietly, and had Mr. Conwell's name cast on the exterior, but when it came to the difficult task of hanging it in the tower they were obliged to call on Mr. Conwell to come and superintend the management of ropes and pulleys.   Then the deep, rich tones of the bell rang out over the surprised old town the triumphs of faith.

> "Ring out the old,
> Ring in the new,
> Ring out the false,
> Ring in the true."

The church was filled from the first opening.   Such continual crowds on church services were never seen before in Lexington.   Mr. Conwell's sermons were profusely illustrated, simple, and showed a liberal spirit toward all christian denominations.   The freedom of every man's conscience from men's dictation, and its dependence on God, christianity a character and not merely a profession, were prominently insisted upon.

His influence was felt outside his church circle, and the old and conservative town awoke to new hope. Other suburban villages were striding forward into cities and leaving the old Battle field of the Revolution sleeping under its majestic elms. Mr. Conwell sounded the trumpet. Progress, enterprise, life followed his eloquent encouragement. Strangers were welcomed to the town. Its unusual beauty became a topic of conversation. The railroad managers heard of its attractiveness and opened its gates with better accommodations for travelers.

The governor of the state [Hon. John D. Long] visited the place, on Mr. Conwell's invitation, and large undertakings were strongly supported. From the date of Mr. Conwell's settlement as pastor, to the present, the town has made astonishing progress, according to the testimony of a great portion of the people. He showed them what could be done, and encouraged them to do it. He practically illustrated the theories of his great lecture "Acres of Diamonds."

One of the town officers writes: "Lexington can never forget the benefit Mr. Conwell conferred during his stay in the community." It is well known that the entire community had Mr. Conwell's sincere affection. He evidently loved Lexington next to the "cloud capped granite hills" of his childhood's home. The law business was abandoned, and his office in Boston finally

GRACE BAPTIST TEMPLE.

·closed. His whole thought was concentrated in the purpose to do good. No one who knew him intimately then could doubt his motives, for the sacrifice was so great, and yet so unhesitatingly made. Buried from the world in one way, but alive to it in a better way. Large numbers of his former legal, political and social associates called his action fanaticism, and Wendell Phillips told him and several friends, one Sunday morning, when on his way to church, that " Olympus had gone to Delphi, and Jove had descended to be an interpreter of oracles." We have received from Mr. Conwell's friends of those days much information in detail which can not be placed in this condensed history. Some of them over praise him, and if he had enemies they do not appear. That such a man would meet with jealousies and even hatred is to be expected. There must have been such things. But he never complained of it, so far as we can learn.

Then followed his ordination to the ministry. He had entered the Newton Theological Seminary, and had begun taking the lectures or studies. The Council of Churches met in the Baptist Church in Lexington some time in 1879. The presiding officer was the Rev. Alvah Hovey, D. D. Among the councilors was the lifelong friend of Mr. Conwell, George W. Chipman of Boston, to whose kindness we have often heard Mr. Conwell refer in addresses. The only objection made to Mr. Conwell's ordination, so far as we can learn, was made by a good old pastor, who said, "good lawyers are too scarce to be spoiled by making ministers of them."

The ordination over, and the Col. Conwell of the past sank out of sight. The curtain fell. The ambitions of public life all disappeared, and henceforth, the homes of the poor, and the rooms of the sick. Henceforth, counselor to the dying, comforter of the mourning, teacher of the humble Christ. In this change he was seconded by his wife, who made no objection to his giving up all for the cause, and starting out with nowhere to lay his head. Never was there a more complete abandonment of things earthly for the Master's sake. But into the privacy of that consecration the historian can go with impunity only after the subject of this biography shall have finished his work on earth.

For the time he gave up his popular lectures, but an impatient public soon forced him back again. He went, however, with evident reluctance. Public scenes and strange audiences became apparently distasteful to him. The pomp and parade of past oratorical victories had no attraction for him more. But more and more the pressure increased, until he again appeared, and is now heard in all the large cities of the country. But, consistent to his purpose, he gives away in charity all and often more than he receives from the Lecture Bureaus and Committees who pay him. He is one of America's self-made men. Such as have been the boast of our nation, and peculiar to our free land.

Mr. Conwell's removal to Philadelphia in 1881 and his subsequent success is so fresh in the public mind that it would be useless to write about it were it not for the sake of preserving the facts for future records.

It was no smiling outlook, in a worldly sense, which took him to Philadelphia. The little church which called him had passed through a broken history. It was not prosperous, and it was but little more than a mission. But it was trying to build a house of worship. It was not in a rich neighborhood. It was poor. We have heard that only twenty-seven people were present when the Grace Church in Philadelphia voted to call him. Few believed he would accept, and it was thought absurd by his friends in Massachusetts. The salary offered him, in view of the difference in the cost of living to him, was considerably less than the amount offered by the Lexington church. The fact that it was a sacrifice, and perhaps because it was a pain, made the change appear reasonable to him. The people of the Philadelphia church were as good and true as they seemed poor and unknown. It was a field requiring work. There was no hesitation or doubt. He accepted the place as soon as he visited it and saw the opportunities for christian labor.

How long it was after the call before he moved to Philadelphia we do not know, but it could not have been long. With scarce an acquaintance in the great city, and many of the church which called him not having heard his name to notice it before they voted, he left all his old friends and associations, all the scenes of his happiest days and plunged into the seclusion of a mission work in a great city. The beginning was crude and inauspicious according to the reports, for he was taken sick, and the church troubled about old debts. But slowly, yet certainly he worked on, full of faith, as he had been in Massachusetts. The poor soon saw a friend.—The young soon found in him a companion. —The dying sent for him at all times of night and day.—Funeral processions sought him until, as mentioned in the *Watchman* of Boston, he attended fifteen funerals in a single week. Almost every denomination sent for him. It was the victory of steady, quiet work, and plain, frank preaching.

The steady but rapid growth of his church, and the development of so many charitable interests attracted the attention of other cities. Many inquiries came to him, and to the church asking for a statement of a plan of work. Mr. Conwell seemed to be unable to answer. "It is a case of evolution," is about all the reply his correspondents get. We have many descriptions of the services and the preacher, but the following one,

written by a Methodist minister in Albany, is quite
accurate and comprehensive :

"I arrived at the church a full hour before the evening service. All the camp chairs were already taken.
Also all extra seats. There was a big crowd at the
front door. There was another crowd at the side entrance. I did not know how to get a ticket, for I did
not know, until I heard it in the jam, that I must have
one. Two young people, who like many got tired of
waiting, gave me their tickets, and I pushed ahead. I
was determined to see how the thing was done. I was
dreadfully squeezed, but I got up to the entrance and
stood in the rear of the pretty church. It was rather
fancifully frescoed. But it is an architectural gem. It
is half amphitheatrical in style. It is longer than it is
wide, and the choir gallery and organ are over the
preacher's head. It looks underneath like an old-fash-
ioned sounding board. But it is neat and pretty. The
carpet and cushions are bright red. The windows are
full of mottoes and designs. But in the evening under the brilliant lights the figures could not be made
out. There was an unusual spirit of homeness about
the place, such as I never felt in a church before. I
was not alone in feeling it. The moment I stood in
the audience room, an agreeable sense of rest and
pleasure came over me. Every one else appeared to
feel the same. There was none of the stiff restraint
most churches have. All moved about and greeted
each other with an ease that was pleasant indeed. I
saw some people abusing the liberty of the place by
whispering, even during the sermon. They may have
been strangers. They evidently belonged to the lower

classes. But it was a curiosity to notice the liberty
every one took at pauses in the service, and the close
attention there was when the reading or speaking began. All the people sung. I think the great preacher
has a strong liking for the old hymns. Of course I
noticed his selection of Wesley's favorite. A little
boy in front of me stood up on the pew when the congregation rose. He piped out in song with all his power.
It was like a spring canary. It was difficult to tell
whether the strong voice of the preacher, or the chorus
choir, led most in the singing. A well-dressed lady
near me said "Good evening," most cheerfully, as a
polite usher showed me into the pew. They say that
all the members do that. It made me feel welcome.
She also gave me a hymn-book. I saw others being
greeted the same. How it did help me praise the Lord!
At home with the people of God! That is just how I
felt. I was greatly disappointed in the preacher.
Agreeably so, after all. I expected to see an old man.
He did not look over thirty-five. He was awkwardly
tall. I had expected some eccentric and sensational
affair. I do not know just what. But I had been told
of many strange things. I think now it was envious
misrepresentation. The whole service was as simple
as simple can be. And it was surely as sincere as it
was simple. The reading of the hymns was so natural
and distinct that they had a new meaning to me. The
prayer was very short, and offered in homely language.
In it he paused for a moment of silent prayer, and
every one seemed to hold their breath in the deepest
real reverence. It was so different from my expecta-
tions. Then the collection. It was not an asking for

money at all. The preacher put his notice of it the other way about. He said, " 'The people who wish to worship God by giving their offering into the trust of the church could place it in the baskets which would be passed to any who wanted to give." The basket that went down to the altar by me was full of money and envelopes. Yet no one was asked to give anything. It was all voluntary, and really an offering to the Lord. I had never seen such a way of doing things as that in church collections. I do not know as the minister or church require it so. The church was packed in every corner, and people stood in the aisles. The pulpit platform was crowded so that the preacher had nothing more than standing room. Some people sat on the floor, and a crowd of interested boys leaned against the pulpit platform. When the preacher arose to speak I expected something strange. It did not seem possible that such a crowd could gather year after year to listen to mere plain preaching. For these are degenerate days. The minister began so familiarly and easily in introducing his text that he was half through his sermon before I began to realize that he was actually in his sermon. It was the plainest thing possible. I had often heard of his eloquence and poetic imagination. But there was little of either, if we think of the old ideas. There was close continuous attention. He was surely in earnest, but not a sign of oratorical display. There were exciting gestures at times, and lofty periods. But it was all so natural. At one point the whole audience burst into laughter at a comic turn in an illustration, but the preacher went on unconscious of it. It detracted nothing from the solemn theme.

It was what the Chautauqua *Herald* last year called a
"Conwellian evening." It was unlike anything I ever
saw or heard. Yet it was good to be there. The sermon was crowded with illustrations, and was evidently
unstudied. They say he never takes time from his
many cares to write a sermon. That one was surely
spontaneous. But it inspired the audience to better
lives and a higher faith. When he suddenly stopped
and quickly seized a hymn book, the audience drew a
long sigh. At once people moved about again and
looked at each other and smiled. The whole congregation were at one with the preacher. There was a low
hum of whispering voices. But all was attention again
when the hymn was read. Then the glorious song.
One of the finest organists in the country, a blind gentleman by the name of Wood, was the power behind
the throne. The organ did praise God. Every one was
carried on in a flood of praise. It was rich. The benediction was a continuation of the sermon and a clos-
ing prayer, all in a single sentence. I have never
heard one so unique. It fastened the evening's lesson.
It was not formal. That benediction was a blessing
indeed. It broke every rule of church form. It was
a charming close, however. No one else but Conwell
could do it. Probably no one will try. Instantly at
the close of the service, all the people turned to each
other and shook hands. They entered into familiar
conversation. Many spoke to me and invited me to
come again. There was no restraint. All was home-
like and happy. It was blessed to be there. Can it
be done in our churches? I doubt it. Human beings
are so apt to abuse such liberty. Ill-bred people would

lose all sense of reverence.   What keeps them in such a balance I can not tell.   But I do not think it would be safe to inaugurate such promiscuous social freedom in many churches.   Yet it is undoubtedly a success there.   The minister engages in the social reunion after the meetings as one of the members, and seems to lose no respect by it.   There is some statecraft back of it, or such a mass of people would go too far.   But the visitor sees nothing but simple plain services and a genial, happy people."

Another writer says : " Mr. Conwell is one of the most eloquent men in our country, but it needs the occasion to develop his power.   He is a man for emergencies, but he has a mighty reserve force which it takes but a minute to fire up.   But it must be a real occasion.   In his hands sometimes an audience is a toy he can toss into any state of feeling, but he don't waste large shot on a small target."

Mr. Conwell's church has grown without any special revival by continual additions week by week.   Summer and winter the interest is the same.   At this time, in in about six years, he has baptized over twelve hundred adult persons.   Many go to him for baptism who unite with other denominations, because of the crowd at his church.   He is liberal in his views, and fraternal with every christian.   There is no conceited bigotry there.

It was after years of inconvenient crowding, and after the city authorities insisted on special precautions

to lessen the danger from the crowd, that the Grace
Church decided to build larger.   Mr. Conwell is said
to have been at one time in favor of a division of the
church into three separate churches.   But no one would
go out of his division, so the people, nearly all being of
the working classes, decided to build.   At the time
these pages are written we hear that the new temple, to
seat 4,200 in the pews, and capable of holding 6,000,
is fast approaching completion on Broad street, Philadelphia.   It will be the largest Protestant church in its
seating capacity in this country.   We believe it will be
no less crowded.

In a French paper published in Philadelphia we find
the following reference to the work and man.

"For eight years he practiced law in Boston, pursu-
ing industriously in all leisure hours his literary studies,
and lecturing evenings in places far away as well as
near.   Since 1870 he has written ten or more popular
books, which have had a very extensive sale.   In 1877
he left the profession of law, with a lucrative practice,
and entered the ministry, being ordained at Lexington,
Mass., in the meantime pushing a special course of
study at the Newton Theological Seminary.   The church
at Lexington was nearly extinct when he first went there
as a preacher, having only about a score of members,
and hardly as many for a congregation, while the house
of worship was quite dilapidated.   In less than ten
months the expenditures for building, repairs and current expenses amounted to $9,835.50, and of that sum

only $1,500 remained unpaid at the time of rededica-
tion.   An enlarged, as well as greatly improved house
was crowded with eager hearers of the new preacher,
and there was soon a threefold increase of members.
In 1882 Mr. Conwell accepted a call to become pastor
of Grace Church in Philadelphia, where advancement
in many respects has been very remarkable.   The
church edifice has been overcrowded, so that it has become inadequate for the accommodation of those de-
sirous of worshiping there, and the list of members has
increased from 190 to 1,200, that church being now
the largest numerically, of any church in the state of
Pennsylvania.   Plans for a new structure have been
accepted, the dimensions to be 107 by 150 feet, the
fronts on Broad and Berks streets to be of brownstone.
There will be four entrances on the former street, and
three on the latter.   The auditorium will be of the
amphitheater style, sloping down from the front to the
rear of the building, where the pulpit will be located.
The side galleries will be twenty-four feet deep, and a
rear gallery sixty feet in depth.   The entire seating
capacity is 4,200, and the estimated cost of the house
is $200,000.   In the main Sunday-school room, there
is to be accommodation for about 1,000 persons, and in
the room for the infant department provision will be
made for 2,500 little ones.   Apartments for social
purposes are to be provided, including a ladies' parlor,
a gentlemen's parlor, a large entertainment room and
a dining-room one hundred feet long, besides a kitchen
and smaller rooms."

The Temple College, for the free education of working men and working women in Philadelphia was origi-

nated by Mr. Conwell, and is one of the most beneficial of the benevolent institutions of our free land. It was founded on the idea that there are many ambitious men and women among the working classes who desire a higher education.

In the first catalogue, issued in 1887, is found the following statement of the reasons for organization of the College. These reasons are written by Mr. Conwell.

"The general objects of the college are to open to the burdened and circumscribed manual laborer the doors through which he may, if he will, reach the fields of profitable and influential professional life.

"To enable the working man, whose labor has been largely with his muscles, to double his skill through the helpful suggestions of a cultivated mind.

"To provide such instruction as shall be best adapted to the higher education of those who are compelled to labor at their trade while engaged in study, or who desire while studying to remain under the influences of their home or church.

"To awaken in the character of young laboring men and women a strong and determined ambition to be useful to their fellow-men.

"To cultivate such a taste for the higher and most useful branches of learning as shall compel the students after they have left the college to continue to pursue the best and most practical branches of learning to the very highest walks of mental and scientific achievement."

At first there were but a few students. No one but Mr. Conwell believed in its success. Even his loyal church had no faith in it. Some of the Baptist denomination ridiculed it, and prominent men opposed it. Some who were interested in other institutions, were openly hostile. All who thought that the laboring man should be kept in his half-bondage tried to hinder the scheme.

He was alone. Being himself a self-made American, he believed many others could do as he had done. He proposed only to assist the young, by showing them how to obtain their own education by their own efforts.

Its success was surprising. He began with one teacher and no organization. But in two years he had eleven hundred students and a completely equipped corporation under the laws of the state. Rich men discountenanced it, and the viciously proud despised the idea of bridging over the chasm between the rich and the poor. But the working men themselves took it up. On Mr. Conwell's birthday, February 15th each year, they give a day's work toward the support of the college, and employ about twenty professors.

The college admits free only those who are actually at work, and is obliged to refuse great numbers for lack

of room.   The classes made most marvelous progress.
Many young men and women outstrip their richer
cousins who spend their whole time at college.   The
Greek, Latin and highest branches of mathematics and
philosophy classes would be an ornament to any of our
oldest colleges.   The graduates must wield a powerful
influence in our nation.   It is a severe test of their
ability and perseverance, which shows unusual mental
and physical power.   They must ultimately be among
America's greatest men.   Such self-taught men, getting
education under great difficulties have been our greatest
pride.   These men have the strength to bear great
burdens.   Mr. Conwell must have seen it, or he must
have builded better than he knew.   No one but Mr.
Conwell had faith to think that when he purchased for
the college, with the payment of a few hundred dollars,
buildings, promising to pay $50,000, that they could
ever be paid for.   But steadily and strongly grew the
favor of good men and women.   The poor took up the
matter.   Little sacrifices multiplied the fund for pur-
chasing, until now no one questions the success of
the college, or the final payment of all its obligations.
Excellent professors of long experience offered their
services at first for a nominal price, and the faculty became one of the most efficient in the country.   The
students study at home, or at their work, and recite
evenings, or by day, as is most convenient.

Many young men from other parts of the country secure work in Philadelphia, and so get the opportunity
for the instruction they need.   Many are studying for
the ministry, some for the law, medicine, science, engi-
neering, literature, banking and the more skilled work
in mechanics and business.   In Temple College they
obtain the collegiate foundation for those professions,
and finish their professional education at other institutions.

To what the college will grow, no one can foresee, or
what Mr. Conwell's plans are for any future extension,
we cannot say.

What a busy life he leads.   Students calling, and
writing for information continually; night and day he
is in demand, visiting the dying and burying the dead;
troubled on every side by unnumbered calls to lecture,
to deliver special addresses or sermons for churches,
charities, missions and different societies; writing books,
preaching regularly to crowds, containing visiting scholars from all parts of the country; examining almost daily
candidates for admission to his church, listening to
countless applications from the poor for aid; watching
over his large church membership and knowing the life
and whereabouts of each one; maintaining a lengthy
correspondence with distinguished men in Europe,
teaching several classes in the college, making wills for

friends, giving business and legal advice to his membership; leading meetings almost daily, and troubled on
every side with book agents, unbalanced philanthropists,
applicants for letters of recommendation, and beggars
of all sorts.   He still labors on easily and good
naturedly.

Poor in the goods of this world, having no pride in
such things, he yet seems to be happy and contented.
That, after all, is worth more than money.   Many a rich
man is poorer in its true sense, than is that busy pastor.
"Trust in the Lord and do good.   So shall thy days be
long in the land which the Lord thy God giveth thee."

RUSSELL'S

LETTERS FROM THE BATTLE-FIELDS.*

From the Boston *Traveller*.

1869.

Port Hudson—Romantic incidents—Soldier dead.

" A LLIGATORS chaw a feller all up," said a little
darkey we engaged to carry our baggage from
the boat landing at Port Hudson to the miserable shanty called by its proprietor, a hotel. "Yes,
Sam, but it's a sleepy time now for alligators, isn't it?"
"Lor bress you, massa, you mus have cum frum de
Norf, shuah, to tink de alligators sleeps. Der yer see
dat ar great whilum pool whar de riber is swinging
them trees and logs and sich around and around. Wall
de federal sojers used to go in dar to wash um, and de
black alligators first boosted dem rite under water with-

---

* These letters are selected from the long series which Mr. Conwell
wrote for the *Traveller* of Boston, and are printed in this volume with his
consent upon the expressed understanding with him that the volume is
not to be published for general sale.—*Ed.*

out winkin at em.   But dose sojers didn't know how to manage um."

"How would you manage one, Sam?" asked we. "Why, I do jist as de cullud folks do down on old Wetherby's plantation.   Ide cotch him by de tip of his tail and jist make him scull me ashore.   Der ye see? When a pussun of color gets an alligator arter him he jist cotches him by de tail, turns it kind a sidewise, so, and de ole feller gits mighty mad dough, but he can't bite de feller what is steerin' him.   An' he has to git, in what direction the steerer says.   White folks cum down here fum up Norf, and de alligators first eat um widout stoppin'.   Put a pussun of culler, he just takes de alligator by de tail and tells um, Mr. Alligator, dis nigger wants ter cross der ribber.   Lend me yer tail, and away goes alligator and pussun ob culler ober to de plantation.   If de alligator spressed his pinion, I spec hede say de pussun ob culler was takin liberties wid a tail de Lord made spressly for de alligator.   But de alligators were made afore steamboats no how."

We rather doubted the feasibility of making alligators perform ferry-boat duty, but as we soon after reached the top of the sandy bluff, upon which our hotel was situated the alligator question was dropped.   After depositing our baggage with a landlady who was as broad as she was tall, and securing a couch on the third floor of the one-story house, we started out to look at

THE TOWN.

There were about a dozen buildings, two of which were grocery stores. Between and around these one-story slab houses ran the ditches and lines of earth-works thrown up during the war. Some little patches of ground between the houses were under cultivation, but the soil appeared too barren and sandy to make a fit return for the labor spent upon it. In several of the ruined ditches, which had not been filled since the war, we saw squads of ragged, dirty children making mud-pies and throwing stones at the ducks. We remarked the contrast between this innocent scene and that when Banks and his men lay out in the edge of the woods yonder. Several men were sitting on the grocery steps, talking about the crops ; and we ventured to inquire, as we approached them, for direction to the national cemetery.

"We don't know nothin' about yer national cemeteries," said a long, lank,

DIRTY SOUTHERNER,

scowling, and making an impatient gesture with his hand.

"I supposed that it was near this place," said we, eyeing another member of the party, who appeared a little better natured ; but, before he could answer, the tall specimen of Southern chivalry arose to his feet in a fury, and demanded of us why we dared to intrude upon a private party, and if we did not know that it was dangerous to tread on a Southern man's heels.

"I do not think I insult any person by inquiring for the grave of a friend," said we, fast losing our temper. "You are a —— Yankee, and that is the worst thing I can say about you! and your room is better than your company," said another man taking the first speaker's part. "Is there not in this company a man who is gentleman enough to tell me where the soldiers' cemetery is?" again asked we, fully determined to stay until we received a civil answer. No one replied. Feeling that this was a free country, and that we had as much right to the grocery steps as they, we sat down beside them, resolved to imitate General Banks's example, who, when he found a direct assault to be useless, proceeded deliberately to a regular siege. While we took up a piece of a barrel hoop and began to whittle, Yankee fashion, they tried to go on with their conversation about the crops, the flood, old Ogleby's mare, and the last fox hunt. But they were evidently uneasy, and their remarks were unconnected, and, at times, unintelligible to themselves. At last the conversation ceased altogether. Some looked at the ground, others eyed us sharply, while our long-haired enemy was trying to whistle "Dixie," and we endeavored to keep time with our jackknife. At last, all out of patience, the company arose to their feet and gathered around in front of us, while one demanded if we wanted to "get into a d——d big fight!" We merely remarked that we had asked all the questions we should, and we were now willing that they should ask some themselves, and kept on whittling. "See here, stranger, I'll bust yer head if yer don't leave," shouted a short man, pushing the others aside, and squaring off before us. We whittled on. "Ain't yer going to leave?" shouted he, bringing his arms akimbo. We whittled as before. "You are a coward, a thief, a liar, a Yankee," yelled he, leaning over to spit the words at us like a copperhead (snake). We whittled faster. "You darsent fight," shouted half a dozen, who loved to see a fight, but acted as though they should not like to be in one themselves.

"Aint yer going to fight?" said our pugilistic enemy. We only whittled. "Come fellers, let's don't fuss any more with him. He's a fool. Let's let him go. He's a harmless Yankee, anyhow," said one starting across the street to the other grocery. One after another they dispersed, leaving us to finish the piece of hoop alone. Soon after

THE STOREKEEPER

came out in a very obliging way, showed us where the cemetery was situated, and hoped we wouldn't mind those red-hot rebels, as the country was cursed by them, and it was not safe for a man to let his Union sentiments be known.   The whole company rushed out of the other grocery as we clambered over the ruins of an old fort, on our way to the cemetery, and rather impolitely wished every Yankee was "buried in the d——d old graveyard out in the woods."

THE NATIONAL CEMETERY

is situated near the edge of the woods, about a mile from the river, and on the very spot where fell so many brave soldiers on the 14th of June, 1863.   But its condition does not reflect much credit upon the United States government, and gives cause for sneers and ridicule to those rebels living near, and they do not fail to take advantage of it.   There are no walks, no flowers, and but an excuse for a flag.   Many of the head-boards have no inscriptions on them, while many graves of known men have not even a head-board to mark the spot.   Nothing can stir our blood so soon to a fever heat as the neglect of the government to protect and care for the graves of its defenders.   Especially where they lie in a strange land, surrounded by a people that hate them and the principles for which they fought. We like whenever we enter a cemetery, filled with brave soldiers, to feel like repeating those thrilling words—

"On fame's eternal camping-ground
  Their silent tents are spread,
And glory guards with solemn round
  The bivouac of the dead."

THE FIELDS

about the cemetery are cultivated in a way that sur-
prises the stranger, and the first question we asked of
the crippled old darkey at the cemetery was in regard
to the ownership of the land. The land for half a mile
around was covered with fallen timber during the war,
which was cut down by the rebels to make an *abattis*
for their breastworks. But it is now cleared and
ploughed under the hand of free black labor, and crops
of cotton and king corn now sway on the plain like the
waves of a lake. The heavy

BREASTWORKS,

behind which the rebels stood when they were able to
repulse the brave attacks of our troops, are still standing, and serve to divide the plantation into sections of
about the right size to let to individuals on shares.
They are, however, gradually sliding down before the
hoe and plough, and in five or six years at most, will be
entirely obliterated.

SECOND LETTER.

NEWBERN, N. C., April 15, 1869.

Many New England soldiers who have spent a portion of their war life upon the shores of North Carolina,
have wished that they were able to make a visit to their

old camping-grounds, and look again upon the scenes so full of thrilling interest. But the transition from war to a state of peace has made such a wonderful change in the appearance of the fields and villages, that the returning soldier can hardly realize that they are the same. Leaving Virginia, now for a short time, to which, however, we shall shortly return, we will wander along the Carolina coast, and note for our comrades the changes that have been wrought since they came here to "fire the Southern heart."

NEWBERN,

in war surrounded by tented camps, long lines of earthworks and forts, with a fleet of gun-boats floating in the Neuse River, was a far different city from the Newbern of to-day. It seems to have become reduced in size, until it is but a miniature of the city we knew five years ago. Then there was a constant tramp of soldiers along the side-walks, sentries on every corner, and jolly crowds in every tradesman's door. Now business is dull and the streets seem almost deserted, while on the corners, in place of the sentries that used then to come to a "shoulder," now lie lazy, ragged negroes, who have just life enough to say as you pass, "Please mister, give me a cent." The wharves that once creaked under the loads of ordnance and quartermasters' stores, where happy-faced sutlers and town merchants received their goods, and soldiers their boxes from home, are now occupied by colored dealers in fish and oysters. The substantial army wagons and ambulances, that were constantly moving through the streets, are replaced by a few two-wheeled carts, drawn by lame mules or "dwarfed cows," appearing as little like the noble beasts we formerly saw here as their drivers do like healthy or prosperous men. The sight of the taveler is refreshed, however, at long intervals, by the appearance of a horse and buggy belonging to some aristocratic North Carolinian or enterprising Yankee. The hospital buildings, so sadly familiar to many of our soldiers, have lost that appearance of quiet and gloom they had during the war, and now, as school-houses or dwellings, look cheerful and inviting. Whole blocks of buildings have been destroyed by fire, and in many places new structures, of a different style have taken the places of old ones. Without the city the change is greater than within. The broad fields, once so white with tents, and the parade grounds, once covered with drilling battalions, are now cultivated by the plough or are left to grow to brush or barren weeds. On the spot where were encamped the 46th and 8th Mass. in '63 the national cemetery now stands, a sad memento of battles and disease. Fort Totten, considered in the confident days of '64 to be one of the strongest fortifications on the coast, has crumbled

away, and the huge piles of sand, which remain of the
lofty traverse, remind us forcibly of some ruined feudal
castle, that has been crumbling for five hundred years.
The line of earthworks reaching from fort Totten to
the rivers on either hand, has, in many places, entirely
disappeared, while in other localities portions of it remain entire. The hand of nature and of man is fast
destroying the landmarks of the war, and in a few years
more not a mound or ditch will be left to tell of the
exhausting toils and weary sieges endured by the soldiers of New England. Yet, with all the change, there
are many familiar localities and buildings in the city
which recall the experiences of camp life ; the large white
house in which General Foster had his head-quarters ;
the long flag staff on an adjacent corner ; the medical
dispensary—the old railroad depot, the now dilapidated
and dangerous bridge across the Trent ; the low house
occupied by Chaplain James and his corps of teachers ;
the numerous negro huts beside the Trent, where were
encamped for a long time the 27th, the 23d and the
21st Mass., and the 9th New Jersey ; the remnants of
barracks near the Neuse once occupied by the 23d, 42d,
17th, 43d and 44th Massachusetts ; the steamer Ellen
S. Terry, on which usually came those welcome letters
from home, and which still plies between this port and
New York ; the old post-office building, on the corner,
still used for that purpose ; together with the many offi-

ces, guard quarters and store houses, tend, in a measure, to bring again a realizing sense of army life. But the

CEMETERY,

with its array of white head-boards, bearing the names of many an old friend and fellow laborer, is the surest and saddest prompter of the memory which the place affords. Drummer boys who beat the *reveille* in time of quiet, and the long roll in the hour of danger, and who went safely through the Virginia campaigns, were conquered by the yellow fever here. A sergeant, honored for his integrity and praised for his bravery at Plymouth and Roanoke, lies here almost forgotten. Private soldiers,—our school-mates and old acquaintances,—fallen in battle or sickness, are placed here, as their head-boards tell us, until the Resurrection Day. At one end of the row are two graves, of which uncommon care has been taken, and to which our attention was called by the keeper. They bear the following touching inscriptions:

No. 1744.
21ST MASSACHUSETTS.
BETROTHED TO C. E. C.

(The name is not given on the board, but we learned that it was a member of Company E, of this regiment). The other reads as follows:

MISS CARRIE E. CUTTER,
BETROTHED TO NO. 1744.
BURIED AT HIS SIDE AT HER OWN REQUEST.

Probably many of the old 21st will know the circumstances and tell the story of these two lovers; but the
inscription on their head-boards is all we know of their
life of love or devotion at death.   But other incidents
we do know that are full of interest to us, and we
doubt not to your readers, which are recalled as we
stand by the flagstaff and read over the familiar names
on the white boards before us: "Follijambe, 10th
Conn."   Ah, yes! that is the very grave they told us
about, and this is the

SAD STORY OF LOVE

they told us.   "The soldier lying in that grave was
reared by kind parents in Hartford, and at the age of
twenty—an honest, intelligent young man—he went to
New Haven.   There he became acquainted with a
young lady by the name of Fenin, who came to visit
her brother, then in college.   They became engaged to
be married, and all was sunshine in the path of life.
But the rebellion came, and she returned to her home
in Harlem, to wait for his return from the war, to which
he was determined to go.   Two years of correspondence
and two furloughs cemented their affection, until they
felt that no earthly obstacle could come between them
and the sweet joys of life in store for them.

But to the loving heart in Harlem there one day
came a report that her betrothed was killed.   In wild

suspense she waited for his letters, but none came. Her father wrote to the Colonel and to the Chaplain. They could only say that he was 'missing.' With no thought of money, or trouble, or care, the old gray-headed father whose daughter, since the death of his son, was his all, searched unceasingly for some clue to the missing one; even venturing within the lines of the enemy. She, with that sublime fortitude which only a woman can command when trouble comes, and with that devotion which makes a woman's love so pure and sacred, shared the dangers and fatigue of a two years' search, knowing nothing, caring for nothing, unless it concerned her lover. Finally his grave was found in the woods near where the 10th once formed a skirmish line, and a little head-board bearing his name carved in crooked lines with a pen-knife, marked his resting place. Word was sent to the mourners, and the next conveyance brought them to the spot. For a while the daughter sat in the carriage, and would not get out; not daring to trust herself within view of the spot where lay the dearest form she ever knew. 'Come, Nellie,' said the old man, and with a forced calmness he assisted his daughter from the carriage. Going to the grave she walked around it—read slowly the inscription—and then folding her hands across her breast, she exclaimed, 'Oh, Charley,' and fell upon the grave a corpse. The old man left alone in this world of grief

was led away by the driver, a maniac. To-day in the
asylum at New York, he is constantly inquiring in his
delirium, why his daughter is not married. Sad, sad
tale. Almost too tragic to believe, yet hundreds attest
its truth." Alas! how many such incidents there have
been since the war, that will never be recorded.

———

THIRD LETTER.

"O now the tide of battle
    Is turned to seas of blood,
When case and grapeshot rattle
    Among the multitude;
And fates, led on by furies,
    Destroy the flying host,
And chaos, mated with despair,
    Makes all the lost more lost."

After visiting two score of battle-fields, and listening
to the thousand and one tales of blood and terror which
the enthusiastic eulogists of each field have told us
about life, valor, blood, death, and bleaching bones,
we had become in a great measure callous to the senti-
ment and enthusiasm which our first field excited. But

GETTYSBURG,

with its shot-ploughed fields and bullet-battered rocks,
—with its broken tree-tops and shattered fences, beside
which the low mound of the soldier still blooms and

fades,—calls up all the retiring host of patriotic emotions which deeds of bravery, martyrs' death beds, with final victory, can awaken.   O ! ye cold, calculating financiers, that would sit down to count the cost and numbers, that can coolly say, there was a battery, here a charge was made, and here a few soldiers died, then go on, and straightway forgetting the spot, come not to Gettysburg.   If you have no heart to swell at fearless patriotism, no soul for praise, no mind for war, no tears to shed, O ! keep your unholy feet from the sacred field of Gettysburg.   Perhaps the

SHADES OF DEPARTED WARRIORS

do not come back to fight over again their battles, as they told us they did at South Mountain.   Perhaps there are in this day no ghosts of men nor aparitions of battling hosts, in earth or cloud to warn us of battle to come or tell of conflicts past.   Doubtless the dead do sleep as quietly as they would in a churchyard.   But to us, in the gathering twilight of that mellow evening the spirits of the long since dead—the faces years ago known and since forgotten ; the spectre forms of the endeared soldiers, clad in Union blue, and girt about with national armor—came from the woods, meadows, hills and fields at the involuntary call of our imagination as they came from the gory fields of Bannockburn and Culloden, at the call of the Highland Seer.   The

long, dull lines of infantry stretching from hill to hill,
—the bright armed cavalry in the fields at the South,
the gloomy, ominous row of light artillery, all came
again and took their stations in the fields, on the hills,
and among the trees.   At Wolf's Hill, the dusty, be-
grimed faces of Slocum's men seemed to lie as they lay
that 3d of July, hugging the earth and firing at intervals
into the woods before them.   At Culp's Hill, Wads-
worth, Geary, Williams, and Slocum again drew up
their lines and again ordered an advance.   How the
woods rang !   The yells, the rattle, the boom-boom, the
fiery flash, the smoky cloud, the crash of the bullet-cut
timber, the bugle calls and commanding shouts, came
from the thick grove as it came that fatal day.   Be-
smeared and bloody faces, torn and dirty uniforms,
broken bayonets and bare heads flitted about from
tree to tree, getting a shot at the foe.   The dark ranks
of the line of battle, some throwing up dirt and logs to
form a low breastwork, while the others filled the woods
with searing lead, worked as diligently in the twilight
as they did the night of July 2d, '64.   Then to Cemetery Hill we went.   But the

PATRIOT ARMY

was there before us.   Howard rode the same sweat-
streaming horse ; the artillery were working the same
dark cannon ; the infantry lay behind the same stone

wall; while down in the valley were the shifting files
of Early's iron-gray division.   How they yelled and
shrieked as they came charging across the valley, up
the hillside and over the walls!   "How the Dutch
scatter!" again repeated Doubleday, as the rebel line
with unbroken front came upon the Pennsylvanians,
drive them from the wall, and rush upon the gunners.

HAND TO HAND,

gun rammer and sponge against bayonets and swords.
"Spike the guns!"   "Surrender!" shout the rebels.
"Never!" "Down with rebels!" reply the artillery
men, as the troops from Hancock come to their support.
The fierce, short battle is soon decided, the rebels flee,
and the brave artillery men soon send their shot and
whizzing shell after the broken ranks of the defeated
foe.   Bang! bang! roar on the guns.   Huzzah! huzzah!
shout on the men, as we hurry over the broken and
scattered gravestones of the cemetery to

HANCOCK'S AND SEDGWICK'S DIVISIONS.

There they are, just as they were that day!   Massachusetts is represented in those dusty ranks that stretch
along the side of the hill, down by the fence, beyond
that clump of trees and on toward Little Round Top.
How firm they stand, how rapidly they fire, how
patiently they wait the coming foe that is just appearing beyond the open fields; how silently they lift their

pieces; how suddenly the storm breaks. How like demons Pickett's rebel lines shriek and gibber on, or how like wheat before a hailstorm they fall, then falter, then flee; while Seminary Hill sends back the echo of victorious shouts,—expect not reader, that our pen can tell. Let them fight on through the dreary, sleepless hours that come, while we hurry on by the ammunition wagons and through the city of ambulances and stretchers to the

DEADLY HILL

of Little Round Top. Here they are again—the fearless men of Sickles's and Sykes's divisions. Here is the battery of artillery, planted in among this almost insurmountable pile of cragged rocks, bellowing in its fury and spitting death and terror from its fiery, hydra mouths. Here are the sharp-shooters, creeping into little niches in the rocks, pushing their rifles through natural loopholes and answering the death-dealing shots of the rebels across the ravine at the haggard, rocky "Devil's Den." Here is the infantry line endeavoring to build a wall to protect themselves from the hissing missiles which came from the peach orchard like hail before a hurricane. Here we can see the whole field, from the orchard around to Culp's Hill. A cloud of smoke covers the front lines, but in the rear are the hurrying stretchers, the hospital colors, the lumbering ambulances, the reserves and supports, all shifting, running, stopping, changing front, lying down, leaping up, bewildering the eye; while the tremble of the heavy guns, the clatter of wagons, the roar of musketry, and the blood-chilling whoop of the horrid shell, deafen and benumb the ear. Oh! he that has seen the battle of Gettysburg will never see the like again.

DEAD FACES!

How they haunt us! Lying all about the fields and beside every tree in the woods. Who are they? Whose father, or brother, or husband? Here is a body all broken and mangled. Who praised the symmetry of that form when last it stood in its native Northern village? Here is a face all black and swollen. Who was it that a few months ago called it beautiful? Here too are

THE WOUNDED.

The house, the yard, the adjoining field is full of them. Over these are the surgeons. "Here, bring that man here. We have no time to examine wounds. We can cut off his leg quicker than we can dress the wound. Bring him along; don't mind his pleading. Lay him on the table. Hold on there, steward." In slashes the knife, harsh grates the saw, and our brother or father is maimed for life. Oh! the maimed and crippled ones of battle! living a whole life of perpetual martrydom. He that is shot and dies, deserves a glorious name ; but what do they not deserve, who are shot and suffer a lifetime *before* they die ?

But let these scenes of battle, like the apparitions they call up, glide into oblivion while we contemplate Gettysburg and its interesting environs by the calm and clear daylight of peace.

THE THRIFTY TOWN.

The town of Gettysburg is now enjoying an era of prosperity which, but for the battle, it would never have seen.   Its hotels are filled with visitors, many of whom like the beautiful valley so well that they will come and settle, bringing with them manufactories, improvements in farming, schools and colleges, that the slow one-cent natives would never have known.   The college build-ings—a hospital at the time of the battle—are now filled with hearty, intelligent students.   The seminary has been cleaned and repaired.   A hotel has been erected at the mineral springs, and business of every kind is flourishing.   We endeavored to find the men who ran away during the fight and came back afterwards to sell well water to our thirsty soldiers ; but, strange as it may seem, even the men themselves denied it.   Only one house in the town was shelled during the battle, and that has been so thoroughly repaired, that it re-quired the closest scrutiny to tell where the shot went through.   But everywhere around the town the

SCARS OF BATTLE REMAIN.

On Seminary Ridge the trees and fences are shattered and riddled, showing plainly how fierce was the contest where the fight began. Here we found

TWO BULLETS,

one driven into the other so far that they could not be pulled apart. The supposition is that a Union and a rebel sharp-shooter aimed so accurately for each other, and fired at so near the same time, that the bullets met, and one being a little more dense than the other, pierced the one coming from the opposite direction. Both fell, of course, to the ground, and thus prevented the death of both the marksmen, which must have been the result had the bullets merely razed each other. When we spoke of this curiosity at the hotel, a whole army of

RELIC SPECULATORS

wished to purchase it. Doubtless the sum which we received for it was trebled when sold to the memento seekers who frequent the town. These speculators do a thriving business in the relic line, and have everything to sell, from a 100-pound shell to the smallest wares of the toy shop, all in some way connected with the battle. Canes cut from Culp's Hill, or Little Round Top are for sale in many shop windows, and if the purchaser is a little incredulous, and inclined to doubt that the canes came from those places, they will march out with him, take any sapling he may select, and make it into a cane in a remarkably short space of time. This business has become one of great importance to Gettysburg, and it is proposed to introduce machinery for the manufacture of toys from the battle-field wood.

THE TRACES

which we found of the fight along the front of Hancock's and Sedgwick's line—except in the blasted peach orchard—were not very distinct, owing to the growing fields of grain and the repairs which have been put upon the few farm houses. But the graves of the rebel dead are there, dotting the fields for miles around. In one or two places the bones were sticking out, but generally their graves were covered with clover, and had none of that barbarously neglected appearance they have in the South.

AT LITTLE ROUND TOP

the bullet scars are still visible on the rocks, while several large flat stones near which officers were killed have been engraved with their names and the date of their death. The stone wall which the troops threw up as a breastwork is still entire, and the trees have not yet outgrown their wounds. At

CULP'S HILL,

our guide pointed out to us the stumps of large trees which were cut down by the continuous fire of musketry, and a long trench in which, according to an inscription on an adjoining tree, sixty Confederates were buried. The breastwork of logs, as well as the trees which lie around, has been pulled to pieces and hacked in every way to get at the tons of bullets which the army left in them. When we were there, the axes of the lead and relic hunters made the woods chipper in every direction. On

CEMETERY HILL,

on the opposite side of the road from the cemetery, the remains of the low earthworks where the heavy guns were mounted are still visible, while the stone walls at the foot of the hill remain as old and moss-covered as they were at the time those fearful charges were made over them. The arched gateway of the cemetery, which is so high and broad that it is used as a dwelling, has been repaired, but the fearful havoc which the shot made with it, can easily be imagined by the visitor who scrutinizes the variegated patches that adorn its front.

THE CEMETERY

has been kept in a neat and tasty condition, the grass being often cut, and the flowers by the graves braced

and trimmed.   Near by the cemetery, in a small open
lot which we passed as we left the gate, was

A squad of about sixty boys, all neatly dressed and
nearly of the same size, were going through the movements of company drill.   It is true that the order to
"shoulder arms by the rear rank" was a little faulty in
the drill master, and that the inclination of the urchins
to poke their long sticks every-which-way at the order
"Right shoulder shift," or to stand upon their heads
upon being ordered to "Ground arms," partook a little
of the funny.   But be as awkward as they might, tread
on one another's heels, or carlessly punch one another's
ribs as they might, they were to us a very attractive
sight.   They were

SOLDIERS' ORPHANS.

War had deprived them of father and mother, and this
large white house beside the cemetery is their home.
"Do you like to live here?" inquired we of a little
bright-eyed, auburn-haired girl that was swinging on the
street gate, near the asylum.

"Oh yes, sir, it is real nice," said she promptly, and
at the same time modestly eyeing her bare toes.

"What do you do here?"

"Oh! we study and sing, and play, and have such
nice times, we girls do," said she.

"What do the boys do?"

"Please, sir, they play with us girls; only they some-times run away down town," answered she, pointing to the military display.

When we had walked away a few rods we turned and saw her still swinging on the gate—singing as gaily as if her mother was inside the house and her father in the field at work. The words "we have such nice times" have come to mind often since, and we have wondered if the old gate on which we used to swing, or the flower beds among which we used to hide,—often much to their detriment,—would have been as attrac-tive if our mother had been dead and the body of our soldier father been mouldering in the next field. We cannot believe they would. We believe that instead of swinging on the gate, or singing "Marching through Georgia," we would have been cowering behind the back door lest the hobgoblins, "ghosts and things," should come from the graveyard and take up their abode by our door for the express purpose of flying away with naughty little boys who couldn't do some-thing possible—be always good natured. We should have thought that our father was in the cold, damp ground and was shivering and chilly. We should have been haunted with the idea that we must die and be put in a box and then covered with dirt, just as father had been—only we were too little to stand it as well as

father could.   How little girls might feel we cannot
tell, as we have had no experience, but we are satisfied
that all boys are near enough alike to feel as we would
have felt and be afraid of the same terrors that frightened us.   Hence we say it is not only unwise but cruel
to place an orphan asylum next door to the graveyard;
and especially so when that graveyard is the last resting place of the orphans' parents.   Some people may
have thought it would be *romantic* to place the asylum
here and send the little innocents from every part of
the State to brood and grow idiotic over their fathers'
graves.   As for us, we fail to see anything romantic or
poetical in it, and regard this spot of all others the
most unfit for the education of children.   Do you think
they will be more patriotic?   Is it necessary if the
father dies in an unjust prison that the children should
be brought up within its walls to make them hate
tyranny? yet it is the same principle.   These children
have enough to eat, good clothes, care, and all that, no
doubt, it is inhuman and exceedingly unwise to keep
them here with the constant reminders of the dead instead of the incentives they should have to an independent and happy life.

GETTYSBURG AND WATERLOO.

When we returned to our room at night with our
mind filled with the incidents of the battle which we

had heard that day, and others we had listened to in other States, we could not fail to see a remarkable similarity between the battle-field of Gettysburg and the field of Waterloo. Many of the charges made by the Confederates were similar in their character and result to those made by the French, and were made over ravines and up hillsides which were the counter parts of those at Waterloo. Le Haye Saint and Hougoumont have their positions on the field of Gettysburg, although no villages mark the location here. Pickett's last charge has often, by the best historians, been placed in the same catalogue with the charge of the Old Guard at Waterloo. The comparison of the losses show that the fighting at Gettysburg and Waterloo had nearly the same result. The allies had 72,000 men at Waterloo ; the Federals 65,000 at Gettysburg. The French had 80,000 at Waterloo; and the rebels 90,000 at Gettysburg. The allies lost 20,000 men ; the Federals 20,000. The French lost 40,000 ; the Confederates at Gettysburg 40,000. The British at Waterloo had 186 cannon ; the Federals at Gettysburg 200. The French had 252 cannon at Waterloo ; and the rebels at Gettysburg 200.

In its consequences the battle of Gettysburg may be counted as important as Waterloo. The former destroyed the power of a well-disciplined and defiant army, which invaded the North for the express purpose

of spreading desolation and ruin, and by the capture of
Baltimore and Washington dictating disgraceful terms
of peace, terms which would have dashed at once all
the hopes entertained by lovers of republics and by the
supporters of free government everywhere.   Napoleon
would have established a tyranny at once destructive of
the interests of the people and the government of
European nations.   Lee would have established a slave-
holding oligarchy or a monarchy, carrying the cause of
humanity back into the centuries long past, and anni-
hilating the glorious work of the world's greatest and
best men.   Gettysburg to Lee, like Waterloo to Napoleon, was a decisive defeat.   From that time, as General
Hood declared to us, not many days ago, he fought
"only to save his honor.'

   While we were thinking of these two battles we could
not resist the temptation to ask ourself the unanswer-
able question : Had the French soldiers loving wives,
sisters, mothers, fathers, at home to mourn them as
they fell ?   Were they missed as our soldiers were
missed?   Did they suffer the hardships of war as
calmly?   Ah ! Of course they suffered,—and were
missed as our friends were missed.   They were mourned
by friends as near and dear as were the Union soldiers
at Gettysburg.   Men are alike everywhere.   How
much of life and history can we learn from a single
battle !

ONE INCIDENT IN THE BATTLE

we cannot refrain from relating: A captain in a New York regiment was ordered to place his company on the skirmish line, without any directions as to how, when or where. The orderly without stopping from a gallop had given the order from the general in command and in the excitement neglected to say "to the right of the Baltimore road." The captain had drawn up his company, which had been detached for sharp-shooting, before it occurred to him that he did not know where to go. Fearing lest he might incur blame if he stopped where he was, ordered a "forward, march," and started for the nearest line, but the colonel in command would not let him pass the line. Then knowing nothing better he counter-marched to his old position near the reserve, resolved to wait orders. None came. The battle went on, from which he had only just been relieved, and his company laid down to rest. Night came and the great battle was over. The captain had lost sixteen men, had fought nobly and was proud of it. But an old enemy, whose enmity he had incurred by superceding him in command of a battalion, and which was the captain's right as he was senior officer, took occasion to say that the captain received orders to go on the skirmish line with his men and refused on account of cowardice. The accuser was a brother of the brigadier. The brigadier preferred charges, and so slyly used his influence that, after its being shown that the order to move was given, and that the captain did not go outside the line of battle, the court ordered a

DISHONORABLE DISMISSAL.

The accuser took the captain's place. Doubtless he was happy. It was such a small matter to hoist himself by destroying the happiness of another, that his conscience may not have felt it. But the dishonored man, what became of him? Ashamed to be seen by a soldier—with all his hopes of fame and life dashed at once to pieces—his good name, and with it everything held dear gone, he wandered about the country in deserted places, almost a maniac, moaning and cursing his unjust sentence. At last a thought full of hope entered his brain, and lifting his head once more, he acted upon it. . "I have been a private soldier before and can be again," said he, and soon after was sent out as a recruit. The year of war passed on; the battles in which he was engaged were many, and as he had his honor at stake he behaved with the greatest bravery. His honor or his death were to be won, and fearlessly he went to his task. The court martial was reversed, and deserved promotion came. One, two, three, four promotions, and he was a lieutenant colonel. At Petersburg a new department was formed, and his regiment was detached from his old corps and sent

into the brigade of his old enemy.   They had not met
since the dark day of that court martial.   The brigadier
was dead, but his old enemy was a captain still, and at
that time under arrest for the third time for drunken-
ness and disgraceful conduct.

When the drunkard learned that the lieutenant
colonel was in his brigade, he sent for him.   Long and
earnestly did the arrested man urge the lieutenant
colonel to forgive him, and after he had obtained assent
he followed it up by requesting the lieutenant colonel
to intercede for him as he feared dishonorable dismissal.
At last the lieutenant colonel agreed to do that and
went at once to the commanding general.

"No, sir.   This is the third time he has been guilty
of such disgraceful conduct, and he shall be punished,"
said the general.

"But, general, may he not be allowed if he chooses
to resign?" urged the lieutenant colonel, resolved if
he could not do the best to take the next best course.
The general hesitated a long time, said that the captain
deserved disgrace, etc., but finally granted the lieutenant colonel's urgent request.   The captain resigned,
glad, indeed, to escape in that way, and returned to
Western New York.   With a brevet the lieutenant
colonel returned to his home, restored, it would seem, to
honor and his good name.   But no; his old foe, who
had asked his forgiveness and received such aid at his

hands, takes occasion to say to all who happen to be strangers to the colonel, " He was dismissed from the service but I *honorably resigned*," and the brave, honorable, benevolent man and officer goes with the stigma still.   When the story was told us at Washington, we thought of other cases that had come under our own observation, and we resolved to be careful how we censured even the dishonorably discharged soldier, lest we might wound a heart already lacerated and broken by the stabs of military injustice.

FOURTH LETTER.

Did you ever see a mean man ?   One with no honor, no sympathy, no generosity, no anything that is good. Perhaps you never have.   But you must not take your experience as conclusive evidence that there are no

MEAN MEN,

for there is no doubt whatever in our mind but that there are some still living.   Not many days ago, and at a place not a thousand miles from Vicksburg, a fierce looking moustache, with a man attached to it, invited us to dine with it.   So urgent was his invitation, and so much of an honor would he deem our company that we consented to go.   We did not wish to accept his invitation, and had much rather eat our corn bread and bacon at the hotel than partake of nature's richest viands in the house of a stranger. Yet there was no such thing as refusing, and so we went.

The moustache stood in the doorway of a splendid mansion as we approached, and condescendingly sent his nigger to open the gate and show us up the labyrinth-like path which led around the flower beds to the porch.

"I am exceedingly happy to see you," exclaimed our host, extending both his hands and almost pulling up into the porch.

"This is my daughter D———, and this my daughter M———," said he, motioning toward some fine jewelry, paint and feathers, supported by two forms that looked for all the world like wasps standing on their tails, but which, in the South, are often called "young ladies." The moustache gave a dignified grin; the feathers bobbed, creases came in the paint, and we walked into the parlor of the chivalrous Southron feeling like an alligator we saw at Baton Rouge trying to climb a tree. However, we soon felt our awkwardness clearing away before the "make-yourself-at-home" demeanor of our host. After the compliments of the day were passed, and we had been introduced to a thin delicate lady with a small voice, a song was proposed, and the paint and jewelry seated itself sideways at the piano.

"Shall I play 'Dixie,' pa?"

"No! no!" quickly responded our host, "give us a national air."

"I'm sure, pa, you must know I can't play national airs; no one plays *them* here."

"Well, give us 'Willie's on the blue, black—or dark —Sea,' that is the next thing to the 'Star Spangled Banner,' isn't it, Mr. Correspondent?"

"We would be happy to hear anything," said we looking over the music, and selecting from the small pile "Sally Come Up," "Up in a Balloon" and "De Skeeters do Bite," wondering if that was the class of music these painted dolls delighted in. These, and the "Bonnie Blue Flag," "My Maryland" and "Dixie," comprised the greater part of the collection.

Soon the usual routine of teasing and coaxing was over and the performer began. We were rather pleased with "Write Me a Letter from Home," and in imitation of the Southern flatterers told the dear performer that it reminded us of Madame Parepa-Rosa. But we did not say "by contrast."

After the singing the conversation turned upon the state of the South. Our host became considerably excited as the discussion went on, and at last arose to his feet, exclaiming:—

"That's the way it always has been. The South is slandered by the North. You say you have been every-

where treated kindly ; and that is, as I know, the testimony of every Northern man that comes here. We
have done rebelling. We say, 'It's all right now.
Come among us ; we will receive you kindly, and do
all we can do for you. Here's my daughters ; as good
girls as ever lived, and not bad looking, either. Now
the time has been when we wouldn't have a Yankee
on this estate. But now—now—the young sprigs are
killed off—and—and—we feel like inviting others to
take their places. We are human. We like society,
and we love our Northern brethren. We receive them
as we do you, sir, with open arms. The people of the
great and noble North are our friends, and we have
nothing but the purest love for them." Here he was interrupted by the tea bell, and we went to the feast of
"good things," determined that if we could not feel
quite at home in that society, we would at least enjoy
one square meal. How we got through the evening
and the night—for we could not break away—we cannot tell. Vague memories of songs, piano, guitar, little stories, the recital of Mother Goose, a cup of coffee
and a soft bed is all we distinctly recall. But when
breakfast was over, which we swallowed in company
with our host only, and we took our leave, which was
exceedingly affectionate on his part, we drew a long
sigh of relief, and rehearsed mentally a eulogy on the
spirit of freedom. We distinctly remember feeling, as

we passed out of the iron gate, which the same colored individual closed, a strong temptation to turn and
inscribe on the panels those classic words,

" Who enters here leaves all hope behind."

If any person had inquired of us then why we felt
as we did, we could not have replied. Everything that
could be done by our entertainers had been done apparently in hearty good will, and as we pondered upon
it we felt slightly conscience stricken for feeling so ill-
tempered. But there are prompters of whom we know
little, whose guidance is much more consistent than
the cold calculations of man:

During our stay in *that place* we met our host often,
and he was always very pleasant and agreeable. We
learned also that he was trying hard to get the office of
internal revenue collector. The morning when we intended to take our departure our friend came down to
see us off, and wished us a happy journey and a long
life, as the train started. Owing to an accident the
train did not get far from the depot, and in company
with other passengers we walked back to the station.
On going into the passenger room to deposit our baggage
we saw our friend, with his back toward us, engaged
in a loud and earnest conversation with a neighbor.
Imagine our chagrin when, as we came nearer to them,
we heard the following conversation almost verbatim :—

" As for me," said the neighbor, " I love the South too much to fraternize with her enemies."

" Nor I, nor I," exclaimed our host, "unless I see that I can make something out of him. The nigger brings a pail of swill, you know, when we wish to catch the pig and get his bacon."

" But what in the —— could you want of that radical from Boston ? " inquired the neighbor.

" I want him to say a good word for me in the radical papers. That's just what I want. I may need them to use in Washington. As for the d—d fool of a Yankee himself, to tell the truth, I felt like cutting his throat every time I looked at him. I would just like to hang up every cussed Yankee that comes down here. For they only stir up the niggers to insolence and deviltry."

" Well, may be you can stomach them, but I can't; and I reckon it will be some time before I'll introduce one, right from Boston, to my young ladies," said the neighbor sarcastically.

Upon this we turned away hastily and went back to our hotel with our minds made up that no moustache, no jewelry, no paint, no waterfalls, no feathers, no sleepy eyes, nor anything would ever get us into another aristocratic mansion where the *pure love of the North* is dealt out for newspaper puffs.

VICKSBURG IN 1860.

The Roman, who could boast of the seven hills and the throne they sustained, was no more vain-glorious than were the aristocratic citizens of Vicksburg in 1860. They were not many in numbers, but they felt as though Vicksburg might at some future day "rule the world." Each family had two servants to each member in the mansion, and hundreds at work in the fields. They could live like princes and do nothing. They lay in bed late in the morning, sat in the shade till evening, were driven out by their servants at night, and returning, danced till midnight. The ladies were too proud to stoop for a handkerchief, and had servants to pick it up and to carry the trail of their dresses. The men, for want of better occupation, walloped niggers, fawned on the ladies and fought duels.

But the

LOCATION OF THE CITY

was hardly pleasant or convenient. Let a farmer place twenty or thirty haystacks on the banks of a river as close together as they can stand, and he will have a *fac-simile* of the h lls upon and among which stood Vicksburg. The streets cut through between these hills were very narrow, and at places were hemmed in by perpendicular banks of sand forty feet high. At other places, where the ravines were crossed, deep caverns yawned upon the dizzy traveler as he dared to look down the embankment. The dwellings and stores were set into the sides of hills or on their tops, while in many cases it was sure death to fall or leap from the porch into the street below. A few brick buildings along the river bank contained the greater part of the merchandise, except perhaps the open spaces where the cotton was piled for shipment to New Orleans.

At that time cotton was king. A Southerner could whip three Yankees. The nigger had no rights which the white man was bound to respect. Jeff Davis often drove up—or, rather, his darkey drove—from his plantation down the river and made bargains with the boats to land at his place to take off cotton. He often took drinks with his older brother, Joe. Jeff talked politics then and tried to induce his brother to go into the Confederacy business. It might do for Jeff, but *not for Joe.* So his brother kept out. Then Southern gentlemen went to Northern colleges for the charitable purpose of showing how they could handle revolvers and bowie knives and how quickly their weak heads could get drunk. Then the white man in Vicksburg was a lord and the blacks were degraded slaves. But, alas! the white man wanted his *rights.* He killed or tarred and feathered all the Yankees who came here ; but it was an infringement of his rights when the rest remained at home. His *rights* called for the enslavement of white and black. He was getting sick of black mothers for his children, and wished to own white ones. He was mad; he was. He hadn't his rights. He *would have* his rights if he had to go up North and whip every Yankee this side of the Canada line. He was spoiling for a fight. He would fight. He would hit somebody, so he would.

And he *did* hit somebody. Unfortunately for him it was a people who had rights they dared maintain. The wave of Southern hate and pride rushed at the rock— burst into bubbles—and floated into oblivion.

VICKSBURG IN 1863.

Three years. Vicksburg in war. A grand sight it must have been. The tops of the numerous hills covered with breastworks and these surmounted with long dark rows of cannon; the Confederate flag, ragged and dirty, flying from the isolated court-house; the long line of gun boats down the river lying listlessly at anchor; the mortar fleet in the river across the penin- sula; the yellow line of earth being thrown from the canal by the United States soldiers; the wide, dark river moving slowly on to the Gulf; the silent city among the hills; the deserted levee and occupied warehouses then under fire; when the smoke of the echoing guns almost hid the gunboats and motar fleet; when shrieking shell descended upon the dwellings, the warehouses, the streets, the hills, the forts,—every-

where; when the smoke of burning buildings curled
up to the bright skies and left a shadow over the city;
when each hill-top belched flame and smoke and iron;
when the city shook until the sandy hills began to
crumble upon the streets and houses in huge ava-
lanches; when all the inhabitants were crowded into
caves dug in the perpendicular banks; when streets
were cut through the hills; when the thick cloud of
smoke encircling the city in the distance showed where
Grant's lines were engaged; and when the dead were
too thick in the streets to bury and the wounded too
many to care for; when death, suffering, sorrow, terror
was the sacrifice demanded of the people who had
transgressed the commands of a just God.   How they
must have suffered!   Living in holes which often caved
in upon them, burying them alive; living on rats, mules
and dogs; constantly in terror of mortar shells, which
fell about the mouths of their caves and often rolled
in to burst, kill and mangle; when legless men, bleeding and uncared for, lay upon the hillsides,—armless
women shrieked in pain for help from the caverns;
when the descent of an avalanche mercifully took from
the inhabitants a few mouths that they would otherwise
have been obliged to feed; when horrid snakes and
lizzards crawled over the sleepers at night; when, at
last, starving and ragged, made insane by weeks of terror and suspense, the general, who had made a " brave

defense," when all but he was starving, surrendered them at discretion into the hands of the "fiendish Yankee." Ah, what a change. "You will have a piece of bread, Massa. Here, missus, take dis habersack of corn bread," says the negro who now carries a bayonet instead of a trail, 'and who waits on "Massa Grant" instead of "Massa Davis." "Dese is good quarters, dey is. Dis was massa's ole mansion, dis was. *Halt, dar!* I'm a sojer; dis in Genel Pherson's headquarters. No, missus, no parties, no nigger waiter, dis day. We're sojers. Dis niggah's stood at dis gate afore. Den I'se licked ef I didn't stay rite yer to wait on de visiters. Now I hev nuffin to do wid visiters; I'se free. I 'list and stan' guard my own accordin'. I'se guard about dese headquarters, so don't hamper dis niggar no more."

VICKSBURG IN 1869.

Vicksburg to-day is a quiet little town of some little commercial importance, and is made lively by the frequent arrivals of steamboats from St. Louis or New Orleans. The buildings show the marks of the great siege, and in many places the patch work covers the greater part of the structures. The hundreds of caves in the sides of the hills are still open and bring to mind the accounts we have read and heard related of the suffering there. Many, however, have caved in, and in some places the whole side of the hill came down into the street at the same time. One of these caves, opened a few weeks ago, was found to contain the bones of a whole family who had been suffocated there during the siege. The cannon have all been removed, but the rifle pits and earth forts still remain on the hill-tops. The spot where Grant and Pemberton consulted upon the terms of surrender, which was then sur-rounded by trees and shaded by the branches of a large oak, is now in a open field, cultivated by a negro who fought there. The marble monument raised to mark the spot was so hacked by relic-seekers that it has been removed and a ten-inch Columbiad gun reared in its place, upon which is engraved the words,

"THE SITE WHERE GEN. U. S. GRANT
ARRANGED THE TERMS OF SURRENENDER WITH
LIEUT.-GEN. PEMBERTON."

The graves of the Northern soldiers, which were thickly strown over the hillsides and along the ravines, have been opened and the bodies taken to the ceme-tery, just above the city on the bank of the river. The Confederate graves are ploughed over and obliterated, while the bones of many are exhumed by lead hunters and carried into the city and sold for fertilizing pur-poses.

"Have you got a lot o' Yankee bones there, Sambo? Well, pitch them in here ; they are just as good as mule

bones," greeted our ears as one of these bone pickers
deposited his load at the shop of the purchaser.   Ah,
don't deceive yourself; they are not Yankee boues;
thank God, *they* sleep in peace, thought we as we
passed on down the street.   The canal, which took so
much time and labor to excavate is now filled with
sand and flood wood deposited by the overflowing
Mississippi.

The Southern chivalry, either refusing "to hire a
nigger" or unable to get them, are now obliged to
carry their own trails, drive their own or borrowed
horses, and turn to the right when they meet a colored
citizen of African descent.   Yankees are working into
the trade and building some new stores ; while the negroes are industrious and happy, having homes and
schools of their own.   A combination of the landown-
ers, who will not sell a foot of land to a negro, at
present hinders the full exercise of their enterprising
spirit; but this cannot last long.   The junk shops are
full of old pieces of shell and tons of bullets, which
will soon be shipped away and recast into stoves, roof-
ing, or perhaps into ploughshares and pruning-hooks.
The glorious old flag floats proudly from the staff over
the national dead and from the top of the barracks in
the city, where the garrison of soldiers now remain.
The silent, smooth old Mississippi moves majestically
on, carrying up and down the commerce of a mighty

nation. No batteries frown from its banks, no rebel flags fly from the bluffs; all speaks peace. That peace which "flows like a river" must soon come, and the nation become the "home of the free," which the soldiers of the nation fought to make it. The Fourth of July was a fitting day for rebels against the government founded on that day to surrender, and may the nation founded in '76 and preserved in '63 see many hundred years before another hand is raised against it.

A SAD, SAD HISTORY.

While we were wandering over the fields to-day in search of the fortifications, picking up fragments of shell, old canteens, bayonet scabbards and pieces of haversacks, we met a man about thirty-five years of age. His clothes were ragged, his beard bushy and uncombed, his hair matted and his face dirty. He was a

PICTURE OF WRETCHEDNESS,

although Fowler would call him phrenologically a smart and intelligent man. He was restlessly pacing about through brush and over the hills, with his hands clasped behind him and his head bent down as if in a deep study.

We hurried up to the spot where he must meet us if he kept on in the direction he was coming, and waited

for him.   He neither looked nor spoke to us in passing
nor heeded our "Good evening, sir," until he had
passed us several paces.   He, however, turned abruptly
about like a man who suddenly discovers that he has
forgotten something, and muttered between his teeth,
"Did you speak to me, sir?"

"We told him that we did, and that we wished to
make some inquiries about the battle-field.   We told
him that we were anxious to see where the Federal
lines were located, as we were from Massachusetts.

"Oh, yes, from Massachusetts," said he, straighten-
ing up; "I have been in Massachusetts, and was born
in Vermont."   Then after a pause he clenched his
hand and said sadly, "I wish I was dead now."

"Why so?" said we, feeling a pity for such a
wretched creature as he appeared to be.

"If you are going out toward the bayou I will show
you," said he, leading the way.

We began to think the man was insane, and after
following him nearly a mile we halted and asked him
how far he intended to go.   He stated that we were
almost there; and so we kept on.   He soon turned off
from the main road into an open field, surrounded by
a growth of young timber; and after passing the barren spot which appeared to have been at sometime the
site of a building, he suddenly stopped, and pointing
to a bunch of rose trees, said, in a low tone :—

"There! In that grave lies the reason why I wish
I was dead. She was my wife, sir."

"How long has she been dead?" asked we as sym-
pathetically as we could.

"Well, seeing you have taken interest enough in me
to come along so far, I'll tell you the whole story,"
said he, taking out his knife to trim the rose bush.

HIS STORY.

"She was twenty-nine years old, sir, and she was a
Southern lady, too. I came down here long before the
war and had a nice bit of land here. I fell in with this
lady at the city up river, and we were married in 1862.
I kept out of the war as long as I could, because I
didn't like fighting anyhow, as I was happy at home,
and because I felt more like fighting, if I fought at
all, among my native Vermonters. I hated the Confederacy, and said so, and it got them down on me.
So one day a company of infantry came along and
said they would shoot me on my own threshhold if I
didn't enlist at once in the Confederate army. I lived
right there then, where you see the weeds. I couldn't
get away from them, and finally, with a gun at my
breast, I said I would enlist, and went off leaving my
wife crying in the door. I can see just how she stood
with her handkerchief up to her face, this way, and
left her a-waving like this. But no use; I had to en-

list with the Missourians, and so I did, with the mental
reservation that I would run away the first opportunity. But I didn't get any chance, for they watched me
as close as a bloodhound does a nigger. Finally,
when Grant's army came down here our brigade was
sent out to kind o' hold them in check. I hadn't
been home since I went away, and my wife wrote me
trying to cheer me up. The second day we moved up
in plain sight of my house, our lines being along
where the fence is yonder. Then the Yankees, they
came out of the woods over there, and began firing.
I wondered what had become of my wife, for the bullets from both sides began to knock the shingles off
the house. One side there, where you see the cellar
door. Well, that's where she went to get away from
the bullets; she and her waiter girl. All night I stood
out there by that tree, wishing I might go and see my
wife. But she didn't know that I was there at all.
But I determined to desert to the Union lines the next
night, so I arranged it to be on picket, and I was set
out there in the corner of the field. Just as it was
coming dark I lay down on the ground, so that the other
pickets might not see me, and crawled along slowly
toward the house, and when I got within a few rods I
jumped and ran for the house. When I came around
the corner a picket discovered what I was at, and fired
after me, and the bullet went over my head. I

screamed, 'Mary, Mary,' and she knew my voice and came right out to meet me on the step, and said, "Oh, dear, dear George, let's hurry away from here,' and opened her arms to put them around my neck and kiss me; but some of the Union pickets thinking there was an advance in the direction of my house opened fire just then—and—and—shot my wife through the heart, and she fell before she had kissed me or I her. The bullet that killed her went through my arm, right there. I took 'her up and ran for the Union lines shouting, 'I'm a deserter,' and they finally let me in, but my wife was dead. The batteries over there hearing the muss about the house began shelling it, and set it on fire, and how the maid got out of the house I don't see. But I came back here when the Union lines advanced and buried her next day, an Illinois chaplain saying the prayers. And that's just why I wish I was dead. I can't do anything nor think of anything but her. Oh, she was such a *good* wife." Here he paused and wiped his eyes with his sleeve, and went on trimming the rose bush. So sad a tale and so real, being in the very place where it happened, brought tears to our eyes in spite of us. We could not find it in our heart to disturb him with more questions after finding out his name, and so left him to pursue our search in the fields beyond. As we were getting over the fence at the outskirts of the plantation we looked back and saw him still there bending over the bunch of rose trees. After traveling in the woods, marking the bullet and shell-scarred oaks, we turned toward Vicksburg, crossing one corner of the field as we went. It was getting dark and the stars were appearing, but we could just see his form leaning over the bush as though he had not stirred since we left him an hour before. We paused upon the old rail fence and said to ourself, Great God, wilt Thou not heal this broken heart!

The incident saddened us, and produced such an impression upon us that we cannot get it out of our memory. We shall retain the impression until our dying day. Oh, that we could do something to alleviate the suffering of that sad heart. But God alone is the only physician who can heal the wounds of hearts like his. May He come, in His infinite mercy, and that, too, quickly.

You say in your last letter that great preparations are making for the

DECORATION OF THE SOLDIERS' GRAVES.

Oh, that we could be there to participate. We should feel a much greater interest than ever before. Don't forget the dead that died and were buried away from home. Dedicate the wreath to them which you hang upon the monument. We have endeavored to make arrangements with the cemetery keepers to have the graves of the Massachusetts and New Hampshire dead decorated with flowers on that day. We would like to have made it universal that no patriot's grave might go without a tribute. But, alas! many will lie in their cold graves unnoticed; but we hope they or their deeds are not forgotten. For ourself we will decorate the graves of our comrades on that day, and strew flowers over as many as we possibly can; and we ask of the patriot assemblies who meet on that day that they remember in some befitting manner the "dead who sleep in a strange land." One hundred and fifty thousand Northern dead lie in the South, and nearly two-thirds of them "Unknown;" you must not forget them.

"He mourns the dead who lives as they desire."

We cannot close this letter without reference to

JEFF DAVIS'S PLANTATION,

which we visited yesterday. It lies on the banks of the Mississippi, about thirty miles below Vicksburg, and is an exceedingly lovely place. Jeff never owned it himself, though he stayed upon it from 1832 until 1861. It belonged to his brother Joe, who lives in Vicksburg and gave Jeff the use of it (or what is more likely, Joe managed to cook up a title when he was pardoned and he saw that Jeff's property was to be

confiscated by the government).   The buildings all remain as they were when Jeff left, except a few negro
quarters that have been torn down.   An old negro
that used to be one of Jeff's slaves, now leases the
plantation of Joe for ten thousand dollars a year, and
hires a hundred and fifty hands to work it.   Not a
white man is to be seen about the place.   Strange
as it may seem to Mr. Davis, his old slave is making
money fast, and feels as proud as any white man "libin
in ole Jeff's parlor dese days."   The whole plantation
of several thousand acres is planted to cotton, which
appears very promising, and from this one plantation
cotton enough will be produced to run a mill in Lowell
for weeks.

"We jist lets ole Massa Jeff make political speeches
an' we'll see dat de cotton grows," said the darkey who
showed us about, and who had a queer habit of showing the whites of his eyes whenever Jefferson Davis
was mentioned.

"Golly, who'd sposed dat dis chile would ben free
and libin on dis yer plantation with my Dolly dar?
Yah! yah! yah!   Ole Jeff cum to grief suah.   He'd
be hoppin' mad, dough, to see dis yer nigger here.
Yah! yah! yah!"

We left him laughing on the shore and moved off to
the boat moralizing upon the mutability of human
events.

FIFTH LETTER.

NEW ORLEANS.

On a floating marsh, that is said to be gradually sinking under its load of buildings, stands the great commercial city of New Orleans. Full of life, every street crowded and covered with the foliage and blossoms of beautiful magnolias and orange trees, it may be said to be the most beautiful city in North America. There are many things in and about it to remind one of French cities, and to justify the claims of its inhabitants, that "it is a second Paris." Beautiful city! Wide avenues, shady walks, grand old buildings, lovely drives, cooling fruit groves, clear sunshine. The spectator of to-day who notes the prosperous streets, the crowded markets and loaded wharves, can hardly realize that these same streets have been the arena of so many terrible combats, or the stage upon which so many fearful tragedies and important comedies have been acted. Canal street to-day, with its decorated show windows, clean pavements, and trains of street cars, has a very different appearance from the spectacle seen there on that other first of May when the Thirty-first Massachusetts and the Fourth Wisconsin Infantry, with Captain Everett's Artillery, marched along the streets, escorting General Butler through the surging mob to the St. Charles hotel. The levee has

a very different aspect from that presented to Farragut's fleet as he moored alongside of blazing warehouses, smoking ruins of shipping and the smoulder-
ing heaps of cotton. The people that appear on the
sidewalks with their gold-headed canes, poodle dogs
and jewelry, have a softer, less offensive look than the
bare-headed, grizzly, dirty rabble that welcomed the
Yankees with threats and imprecations. The dark,
deep river that threatens each spring to overflow its
banks and come down into the basin occupied by the
city, bears to and fro a hundred steamboats where
drifted then the frowning flagship or threatening gun-
boat.

1862.

When we left the train which brought us from Lake
Pontchartrain we almost expected to see the same men
and witness the same scenes which occurred in 1862.
We well knew they would not be there; but all our
previous ideas of the city had been so interwoven with
thoughts of insurrections, mobs and battles that the
simple mention of the name called up the scenes of
war. Then the streets, the old custom-house, the
statues of Jackson and Clay, the Saint Charles Hotel
and the crowded markets, all served as a connecting
link between the present and past,—shadowing the
events of the past through the scenes of the present.
One needs only to walk up Saint Charles or Poydras

streets and see the handsome faces that adorn the latticed windows or the beautiful forms that grace the sidewalk, to be reminded of that

ARMY OF LADIES,

who, pistol in hand, rushed through the streets on the 29th of May, crying, "Burn the town! Destroy the city! Don't mind us!" Beautiful dolls in time of peace; almost indispensable as parlor ornaments in time of prosperity, but rather poor material for fighting in time of war. We have never heard that a single one of this host of armed Amazons ever mustered sufficient courage to discharge a revolver. But they were a power then. From street to street and house to house they ran with dishevelled hair and flushed faces, stirring up the spirit of chivalry and rebellion. But the horrid men wouldn't come up to the scratch. The "fellers" had seen too many artificially red faces and too many towzley curls draggling down the ladies' backs before to be stirred by them to deeds of valor in the presence of Farragut's fleet and the corps of foreigners. So the dishevelled-haired, red-faced dodge become a failure, and the sweet dears went home to comb their hair and fix up to receive the Yankees. The next day

THE YANKEES CAME.

The city was hid in a huge cloud of smoke. Buildings were burning, women were flying to the country and Canal street and levee were packed by a furious, uncontrollable gang of "plug-uglies," whose occupation had been gambling and fighting, and whose present desire was to murder and assassinate. From the great ships came the blue uniforms, the bright bayonets and pavement-shaking artillery, and forming on the wharf, pierced the crowd and wound up Poydras and St. Charles street to the hotel.

GENERAL BUTLER WAS THERE,

marching coolly along between a file of soldiers, the object of everybody's attention. Brave man! A general in battle has the excitement of the rattle, the yells, the booming and the smoke to lift his courage and take his thoughts from personal danger. But he who can deliberately, without hesitation or fear, march through an army of infuriated roughs that is seeking for any little chance to shoot or stab him, with his sword in his sheath and his revolver in his belt, can be none other than a *constitutionally* brave man. He that could sit unconcernedly in his room while the mob were crying for his head without, and while his best defenders gave up the city for lost, and could order the artillery to open on a crowd of a hundred times the number of the garrison without a doubt as to its results, is someting more than an ordinary man. General Butler may have made some mistakes in his life, but his behavior at New Orleans is surely not one of them.   General Butler is gone and

THE MOB

that threatened him are gone.   But, as in almost every other instance, the general has outlived his enemies and their machinations to injure him.   If one should write a history of that crowd since the soldier citizens of New England and Wisconsin heard their threats of vengeance, he would concentrate into a few pages, many of the most henious crimes ever committed; thousand of murders, rapes, assassinations, robberies and street brawls, such as the records of crime never before saw in so small a space.   We doubt if ever in the history of the world there was such an army of the vilest, lowest, most beastly men of earth gathered in one city.   The knife, pistol, club or gallows, has, however, disposed of them, and the city is quiet now. Beautiful city!   Not a trace of war!   So prosperous, blooming and happy!   Who would suppose that it could harbor so many thousand villains and murderers?

With all these thoughts passing through our minds we sauntered about the city in company with several army friends, looking for those places and buildings whose fame the history of the Rebellion has made immortal.

THE CUSTOM-HOUSE.

Into the uncompleted custom-house, upon which General Beauregard was working when he abandoned architecture for the field, we went, admiring the grand design and the ponderous masonry of the building. In the rooms where the troops were quartered during the war, we found the desks of busy clerks surrounded by piles of official papers and bundles of red tape. In the basement was the post-office, occupying nearly the whole floor, and its entrance filled at all hours of the day with an anxious-faced crowd. On the second floor, the way to which is up the same old rickety plank stairs, is the room occupied by

GENERAL LONGSTREET.

He was there when we went in and greeted us in a very cordial manner, appearing as much at home as any other man should in a fat custom-house office. If a man ever has reason to smile, it is when he gets into the custom-house. For it is one of the neatest, prettiest, jolliest, laziest, wickedest positions ever held by man; more pay, more cigars, more sweetmeats and fruits, more bribes, more salary than any other office affords, and at the same time requires less work, less care, less hours, less knowledge, less everything but political chicanery than any other business in the world. So General Longstreet likes it. But as the fact that a man is a custom-house officer does not necessarily indicate anything in regard to his character, and as it has been whispered of late that some tolerably good men have gained admission to custom-houses, we will take it for granted that General Longstreet cared nothing about the few thousand dollars a year or the "perquisites," but accepted the office merely to show the world what a sacrifice a rebel general could make "for the good of his suffering country." Poor man! How we pitied him as we noticed his surroundings and thought how much happier he must be at home, doing nothing. Oh! it stirred our heart to its lowest deep to think of what this man might have been had he never forsaken his country or commanded a "rebel squadron." Before he took up arms in that cursed rebellion he could have followed almost any profession,—dry goods clerk, blacksmith, or groceryman,—and had good pay. And now, here he is! How sad! Doomed to pass nearly three hours every day in the custom-house, surrounded by cushioned sofas, easy chairs, damask-hung windows and Brussels-spread floors, with clerks running in to announce visitors or bother him with decanters and bottles; obliged to drink at everybody's invitation; to smoke the best Havanas at other people's expense; ride out every evening with his family in an importer's carriage-and-four; and absolutely forced to draw his

$10 a day or disappoint the secretary of the treasury by leaving it in the paymaster's hands. Sad! sad! When we noticed his long slick whiskers, his round face, plump form and lively manners, and saw how his room was made hideous with cigar boxes, wine bottles, fruit crates, and downy settees, the bottom of our heart was again turned topsy-turvy, and we resolved never, never to go into the rebel army, never to shoot Yankees, never to take afterwards the winning side, if it must come to a fate like this. It seemed as if our host knew our thoughts, for as we went in he glanced around. as much as to say, "I know it is hard. You hardly expected that I would ever come to this. But it is all for the great and glorious Union." However, the general kept up good spirits, and congratulated Boston upon escaping the odium of having one of her own citizens appointed as collector of customs for the port of Boston, He hoped the war was over, and prayed for peace. We told him we thought his prayers would be answered, and then left to make a call on

GENERAL HOOD.

We found him in a one-horse commission store on the second floor of a stone building on a side street. He was very sociable and talked freely about the war and said he regretted nothing he had done, and would do the same fighting over again if he had a chance.

He said when he succeeded General Johnson in command of the Western Confederate army he knew the
game was up.   He was only fighting to save his honor.
The "revolution" was crushed when Vicksburg fell,
and he said so at that time.   He said it was painful for
him to talk about the lost cause, and he did not like to
recall the war.   We came near suggesting that if he
could get into the custom-house it might cure his
squeamishness on the subject of the late unpleasant-
ness, but as he said he should never make any
political speeches we concluded he was too far gone
for a custom-house cure.   He arose on his crutches
as we left, bidding us good-bye with an emphasis
which indicated that he would like to have us call
again; so we have kept a good opinion of General
Hood.

GENERAL BEAUREGARD

received our formal call in that dignified manner which
all men who have "had greatness thrust upon them"
usually display when they come in contact with the
smaller portions of the Almighty's universe.   He was
very condescending and "granted us a short inter-
view."   He is president of the New Orleans & Jackson
railroad and has his office in a fine marble-front
building in the wealthiest part of the city.   He made
little or no reference to the war, but confined his con-

versation to the commercial convention and the condition of the railroads. From what he said and our own
experience we concluded that nearly all the railroads
in the South were almost as bad stock to invest in as
Southern Confederacy bonds. Nearly every one had
borrowed money at the North before the war, and
when the Confederacy confiscated all moneys due
Northern creditors they paid these sums to the " powers that were ; " and, being now obliged to pay these
debts to the lawful creditors, they have become poor as
a church mouse. Beauregard was made president of the
railroad because the people along the line were rebels,
and the road would be more popular with a rebel general at its head. Again we resolved never to be a rebel
general if such misdemeanors would inflict upon us the
hard task of drawing a big salary and doing nothing
for life as a railroad president. As we did not deem
it such a " tremendous honor " to wait upon the man
who had caused so much needless bloodshed, and as he
seemed to think we were favored with the smiles of a
great and noble man while we remained in his office,
we thought best to bid him good-bye. He invited us
to call again whenever we came his way, which we
may possibly do, if by that means we can get a free
pass over the New Orleans & Jackson railroad. From
General Beauregard's office we went to the outskirts of
the city to see how fared

THE CANALS AND DRAINS.

which General Butler ordered dug when he kept the
pestilential yellow fever out of the city. We found
them partially filled with filthy mud, while the top of
the black water was covered with a thick scum of a
yellow-blue color. The stench from them was nearly
suffocating, and we made haste to get on the windward
side to avoid a retreat toward the city. The city is on
a marsh that is much lower than the river, and stag-
nant water would stand here at any time of the year,
making it sickly if there were no other aggravating
causes. But when the offal and filth of the city is
carelessly thrown into these fever-breeding sloughs and
left to decompose, the effect is terrible. One of the
most rabid rebels we have met in the South went with
us to visit the suburbs, and although he said all the
bad things and told all the lies he could get into the
hour we were with him about

GENERAL BUTLER,

yet when we asked why the city was not kept as
neat and these drains as clean as they were during the
military rule of General Butler, he expressed his idea
of the incompetency of the city government in very
strong terms.

"I heartily wish he was back here," said he, "to pull
these city officials over the coals. Why, the only

healthy year this city ever saw was when he was here
to make these lazy fellows toe the mark.   As much as
I hate him I wish he was back, and would vote for him
in a minute."

"I hardly think he would run well for mayor," said
we, jokingly.

"Yes he would though," said he.   "The people
would all vote for him just to spite the present incom-
petents."

Later in the day, after we had returned to the Saint
Charles Hotel, we had some conversation with another
hater of Butler, and when we referred to the recent
action of the Legislature in

LICENSING GAMBLING HOUSES,

lottery schemes, and such places, he exclaimed: "Well,
after all is said, Butler did do one good thing for the
city in suppressing crime.   You may not believe it,
sir, but he renovated this city, and a rowdy dared not
stay here.   Really I wish he could be in command
here long enough to clean out these gambling dens."

So it was everywhere we went.   Men cursed Butler;
wished him all manner of evil; wanted to fight us for
refusing to "see it in that light;" yet each admitted
that he wished the general was back to summarily
cure some evil they hated.   But no two agreed on the
same thing.

A WEALTHY NEGRO.

One day as we were wandering around the suburbs of the city looking for magnolia and orange blossoms, we found a stout negro, about thirty years old, digging away in a very large field. He asked us the time of day, and we turned to talk with him. He seemed very intelligent, and told us that he could read and write. After learning that forty acres of this very valuable land belonged to him, we inquired how he came to buy it.

"I tell you," said he, "it was mighty hard work at first; but I got a little and saved a little. I bought two acres and the next year paid for three more, and so on until I got forty acres. Land was awful cheap then. But now I couldn't earn enough on my whole forty acres to buy another acre; it has gone up so."

"Does any of this land alongside here belong to colored men?"

"Oh, yes! Lots and lots of it. You see long ago General Butler was down South and he told us colored folks this way—says he, 'The colored folks are going to be free. They must be free. Now if they will learn to read and write, they will be practically men and women like white folks.' Then he said, 'If now you will go to work and earn, no matter how little, and lay it by until you get a little more, and then buy land, as you will some day, then you will be free like white folks.' He said a darkey with no money was mighty poor, but if he had money and land he would be as good as other folks. So, you see, some of us, with nothing but our hands to do with first, said we would try it. And after trucking and working at the cane and potatoes we got a little, and when we see the chance we got a white man to buy for us; and now here we are. One man over there on the shell road is worth fully thirty thousand dollars. His land has gone up so."

We wished him much success, and went on with our search, thinking what a condition the country would have been in had there been no General Butler. Cross out his work, and what would the war have been?

At one of the hotels in New Orleans we met a company of Northern health-seekers, and among them was a member of the Fifty-second Massachusetts, who was

TRAVELING FOR HIS HEALTH.

He was well acquainted with the city, and we went out to the old camp-grounds together. But the cotton and sugar then covered the spots and it was with difficulty that we found them. With him we visited the ruins of Forts Jackson and St. Philip. But he was almost exhausted on our return, and before two months had passed he was sleeping the sleep of death. His name was Matthews, and he resided in New York. His health had been impaired in the army and he was in hopes that a second visit to the old scenes would give him back the health they took. Alas! how many there are yet lingering, dying gradually since the war from diseases they contracted then—all the more martyrs for suffering three years of dying instead of so many moments. Yesterday we laid our only brother in the cold grave. He was a soldier. Refusing promotion, although repeatedly offered it, he plodded nobly on, doing cheerfully the work of a common soldier until he was almost forced into a better position. Disease came upon him, as it did upon so many thousand others, slowly and surely. Four years he lingered with us, never murmuring or regretting his service, and to-day the great craggy mountains that surrounded the home of his birth look down in silence upon his new-made grave. Charles has passed over, and bound us by one more pledge to ever hold sacred the principles for which he gave his life.

THE NATIONAL CEMETERY,

in which are buried all the soldiers who died in the department of Louisiana, is situated on the old New Orleans battle-fields, where Jackson fought behind cotton bales. At the time we were there beautiful